A New Beginning

A New Beginning

S. Marshall Kent

ARCHWAY
PUBLISHING

Archway Publishing books may be ordered through booksellers or by contacting:

Archway Publishing
1663 Liberty Drive
Bloomington, IN 47403
www.archwaypublishing.com
844-669-3957

ISBN: 978-1-4808-7644-6 (sc)
ISBN: 978-1-4808-7645-3 (e)

Library of Congress Control Number: 2019914843

Print information available on the last page.

Archway Publishing rev. date: 11/30/2022

Contents

BOOK 111 CONT.

BOOK 1111

The End of a Trilogy

S. Marshall Kent

"And I Remember" was S. Marshall Kent's first published books. It came in the form of a trilogy and "A New Beginning" is the conclusion of the Wilson Family's story.

I have yielded to a "History" of concerns for the verses, and the edification of styles that haunted my desire to writ. I lack the artistry of the accomplished, successful writers; still I have learned that life created "style changers" in everyone.

These books are an attempt to personify the need, value, and appreciation of continual communication. I have attempted to expose the torment and results of living without it.

The trilogy deals with the lives of the Wilson Family for four generations. It attempts to delve into their minds and expose their frustrations, struggles, and heartaches as these events changed personalities, attitudes and lives forever.

The story of the Wilson family personifies the journey of human fear, emotions, death, sorrow, rape, greed, and rejection. An attempt is made for the reader to recognize some of the situations, dialogue, results, and mistakes as a way of relationship awareness.

The events strive to reveal the inner strength of those who are resourceful, perseverant, understanding and forgiving as they seek harmony and love.

The names, characters, events, locations are derived from my still growing imagination. To escape the wrath of authors prolific in their craft -who would dare I encroach on their perfection: I ask your indulgence, as I continue to master my style. For, I seek not to misguide my thoughts into conformity,

S. Marshall Kent - is retired, a late bloomer as a storyteller seeking to expose years of dreams that glisten at the idea of giving them "life."

BOOK 111 CONT.
A NEW BEGINNING

Chapter 1

Life Changes

With Kurt and Ava now married and moving into their own home soon; Greta wanted something to re-focus and re-kindle her intellectual interests. She loved the years spent raising her daughter but now, with Ava married, those days were over. Greta wanted something to keep her mind alert and give her life new meaning and purpose. At fifty-one years old, an avid reader, she was quite attractive, energetic, and religious about keeping herself physically and mentally fit; always eating healthy foods and exercising regularly.

She signed up for a local adult education five-week seminar called "Thinking Out-side the Box" sub-tagged as "Things to Do and Consider for Empty Nesters."

Attending two weeks of classes, Greta was disappointed; games, travel, and hobbies were the professor's suggestions. Greta traveled half the world in her younger days as a reporter. What she wanted now was to find a way to rekindle her spirit; give her the determination--she once had- only as an older, wiser, person. The world has changed, and Greta had changed. She was no longer the same person as she was before Slade West and Ava; her views changed along with how she viewed life, and the issues presented. Greta was looking to regain the independent drive, creative motivation and self-satisfaction, she previously enjoyed. Despite having authored forty major bylined articles during her years home raising Ava. Greta felt she needed to dig her teeth into something that would light her fire—but what?

However, before Greta could pursue her own interests and future, there was another matter pressing that needed her attention.

Chapter 2

Unexpected

Aunt Rita's granddaughter Mary Jane would be graduating high school shortly. Greta spent hours on the telephone with Katherine, Mary Jane's mother and Rita's daughter. Those discussions were about the graduation present Greta wanted to give Mary Jane.

Mary Jane, and Greta's daughter Ava were close friends despite Ava being eight years older. Greta wanted to take Mary Jane on a five-week trip to Europe visiting five countries.

Katherine felt Greta too permissive a parent; she was aghast at Ava's worldly knowledge and exposure at an early age. Greta persisted discussing the history value of such an exposure. In time, Katherine, and her husband

Jeff, gave up arguing. They agreed to arrange a Passport for Mary Jane and allow her to go Clayton for a week before the European tour with Greta.

With her parents' permission, Greta booked the trip to Europe taking in Rome, Paris, Madrid in Spain, Germany and of course Switzerland. Mary Jane's often spoke about her interest in designing clothes. So, now her parents in check, three weeks before graduation, Greta announced to Mary Jane her "special graduation present of a five-week all-expense paid trip touring places in Europe!"

The girl was overjoyed. Greta mentioned the trip would provide her an opportunity to see not only the different clothes worn in each country but also to compare the different architectural designs as she learns a bit of the history in each country, along with enjoying the different foods. Mary Jane was happy but concerned; Europe—Paris—Rome they were all romantic places where she did not want to look like a high school student. She would not feel comfortable making that kind of an impression. She wanted to appear as a mature young college woman. Aunt Greta assured her she would help. All Rita's children called Greta "Aunt" out of respect.

Katherine and Jeff agreed to allow Mary Jane to arrive in Clayton a week prior to their scheduled trip. Greta felt within the week she would be able to take care of all Mary Jane's concerns. Greta knew this trip would create an awakening of a world Mary Jane's formal education did not supply. It would also give Ava and Kurt the time alone needed, while living in Greta's house, until the renovation of their residence is completed.

The only thing left for Greta to do---before the trip with Mary Jane---was to complete her adult education course.

Chapter 3

Unfinished Business

The instructor for the course "Thinking Out-side the Box" was Richard Hamilton. After the death of his father, four-year-old Richard and his mother, Martha, moved to the United States.

His mother met Edward Hamilton when she was out with mutual friends in New York City visiting an art museum. Mr. Hamilton was on a business trip at the time; and joined her group for lunch. At the luncheon he invited Martha, to bring her son Richard, and visit him in Clayton to attend their renowned art festival.

The Clayton art festival was known throughout the state as an opportunity to explore diversified artistic wares, meet several of the young artists, and be able to purchase rare finds. Several telephone calls lasting over a period of four weeks Edward Hamilton convinced Martha and her son Richard to arrive in time for the Clayton art exhibition.

They were invited to stay with Edward at his mother's home; but not feeling comfortable imposing, they stayed at the new Clayton Hotel for their ten-day visit. Mr. Hamilton took the opportunity to show them the benefits of living in Clayton. He took them both to dinner, introduced them some of his friends and showed them around the area touting the benefits of raising a child in a friendly, beautiful area. It was obvious that Edward and Martha were enjoying each other's company. Martha toured the area with Richard in tow and decided it would be the type of community good for raising her son.

Edward Hamilton helped her find an apartment, with a short walk to school for Richard, and even a job for Martha. Eight months after their move to Clayton Martha married Edward Hamilton and the family moved into his mother's house. Mrs. Hamilton passed away years prior to their wedding. Edward Hamilton was her only child and inherited her home. Martha loved the three-bedroom, 2300 square foot house. The older stately home had a two-car garage and a beautiful front porch and back yard for Richard to play.

Edward and Richard became friends with their move to Clayton. The boy had just turned six-years-old when Martha and Edward married. Edward adopted the boy shortly thereafter and the two became remarkably close. Richard became their only child.

Through their relationship Richard looked up to his "father" who was a teacher. Once in college Richard became a teacher. At sixty-three-years-old Richard Hamilton stood 6'4" tall, with brown eyes and thick gray and brown hair. Divorced, Richard Hamilton was quite taken with Greta; having read her a few of her articles in the past, he wanted to get to know her much better.

He made attempts to date Greta, but Greta was not interested. To humor the man, she agreed to have coffee with him after the last class. When the last class was over, Greta and Richard Hamilton went to the small coffee shop, around the corner from the school.

It did not take long into their meeting for Greta to be bored. All Richard spoke about was raising his two sons alone, the number of teaching awards he was given and, his divorce saying, "His wife just was not ready to raise children. She moved to another city, gave him custody of the boys then two and four years old, and never visited them again." Greta thought: *He was obviously a good man who raised his sons alone, gave them a college education and never married. Both his sons were married, and they each had two children. Richard appeared a nice man, but he was not Slade West.*

Her thoughts often went back to Slade West and their time together. When that happened, she realized how great falling in love with Slade felt. She regularly recalled those emotions. Slade was honest, gentle, caring, smart, efficient, handsome, a great cook; and a man with integrity who knew the value of appreciating loving someone and being loved in return. If only…

Class over, coffee over, Greta thanked Mr. Hamilton for a "good" course and inviting her for coffee. He asked if she would have dinner with him on Saturday, but Greta said, "Thank you, I am taking your sage advice; 1 am leaving for Europe soon, heading to five countries. I'll be gone a while. I wish you all the best."

Chapter 4

Anticipation

It was time to begin preparing for the trip to Europe with Mary Jane. Greta would be revisiting the countries she toured with Ava. She thought: *It will be interesting to see the excitement and thrill of a young girl as she views the pleasures introduced to her of a different world that opens through travel.*

Greta excelled in exposing Ava, at an early age, to parts of the world. The child loved traveling and was a sponge taking in bits of history about each country and learning a few words in the language of the people at every stop. Greta was her guide, writer and teacher. *I can't believe how excited I am about this trip. Well, once again, I have the opportunity of educating, exposing and observing how a -not so young person- grasps the wonders of a world she has never seen before. I will be the first to observe her amazement and awe. I guess, it is reasonable that I too, am anxious and excited.*

Chapter 5

Original Plan

Greta was leaving the country without telling Ava she had a trust fund. Her plan, from the beginning, was to raise her child providing a broad educational background, a sound value system, with appreciation, and respect for everything she has including money. In this way Greta expected to feel assured her child would be able to manage what was eventually coming to her from her father's trust fund. Greta's plan was working except…

Greta was a good teacher. She made sure to go over expenses and costs to awaken in her child the desire not to squander or take money for granted; and to take care of her possessions. Ava always believed they were living solely on her mother's residual payments as a writer. She was never led to believe anything else. While in high school, like other teenagers, she had a part time job and even worked while in college.

When Ava wanted to spend on something a bit too expensive; mother and daughter again discussed finances. It was at these times Greta's confidence was bolstered about Ava's handling of money; the girl budgeted, appreciated opportunities and took care of her belongings.

All this changed when Greta met Kurt. It was obvious from their first meeting Kurt did not have same value structure. Kurt's parents died when he was twelve years old, and his bachelor uncle obtained custody of him. The boy, now living with his uncle, gave his uncle's life new purpose. Kurt had three friends in high school, and rarely did things with them. Kurt never had a job while going to school; his uncle gave him everything he asked for or thought the boy should have without giving him any guidance suggesting responsibility. Kurt wasted money on frivolous things and did not use his time wisely. He barely made his grades. In Greta's eyes, the young man had little potential for success.

Ava had a dozen good friends, always busy doing things with them; and was the life of the party. However, after meeting Kurt her free time was spent with him; in fact, from the time they met, Ava never dated or went out with anyone but Kurt.

When Ava graduated from college, Greta wanted her to teach for a while and meet other people, experiencing, more of life. But Ava surprised her, as soon as she and Kurt graduated from college, all Ava wanted to do was to marry Kurt.

Unable to change her daughter's mind she provided Ava and Kurt with a beautiful wedding, and a honeymoon for a month in Paris all paid. Great grandma Betty left Ava the family house in Clayton along with extra money to renovate and update the house. Honeymoon over, the kids decided to renovate the house; planned what they wanted and hired the contractors to begin at once.

Ava wanted to live in the house Betty left her more than anything. Kurt agreed. Two weeks after they returned from Paris the renovation began.

Greta saw how both spent money during the wedding and with their purchases for the renovation. It confirmed her fear; it was not the right time to discuss the trust fund with Ava. Greta was concerned they might take the money for granted and squander it. Greta felt Kurt lived in his own world. She mentioned to Ava that she already had a teaching position, but Kurt still had not even looked for and did not have a job. Ava assured her she could deal with the situation. Ava secretly hoped things would work out fine; but she knew it might take time.

Greta was leaving the country, and leaving Ava, she called Mr. Cantor in New York and mentioned she would be traveling out of the country for five weeks. Years ago, when Ava was young, she made a will. Her will stated that her brother Michael would be Ava's guardian until the age of twenty-two should anything happen to Greta. Even though Ava is close to being twenty-two, she has never revealed to Ava that she had a trust account. Her brother knows all about the trust and he would notify Mr. Cantor should anything happen to Greta while traveling.

Chapter 6

Family in Need

Earlier this year, Greta's Aunt Rita mentioned that her daughter Katherine and her family were having a bit of financial difficulties. "Jeff, (Katherine's husband,} was out of a job for eight months due to his company merging; the family lost medical and dental insurance not counting salary as ninety people were let go. When Jeff needed emergency gallbladder surgery; they did not have medical insurance, it put the family behind in all their payments. They recently applied for a loan against the house to send Mary Jane to college and catch up on their bills. But they lacked the processing application funds. Katherine is working but with one car, and young son who would be alone after school, she had only a part time job."

Rita said: Carl's burn creams have been well received and he is successful in the United States. He has

just began traveling to other parts of the world to pro-
mote the creams. He knows little of what has happened
to Katherine and Jeff. When Carl is home, he has limited
time to get ready for the next series of lectures before
leaving again. While I try to bring him up to date on all
our children and grandchildren; it is hard to burden him
with these issues. Considering there is, Shana with four
children, Katherine with two children and Joseph Carl
with three children.

What Carl gives our children is generous. He was
brought up to believe money was for achievement and
holidays. Carl gives to the children for success at school:
Birthdays, Graduations, Holidays like Easter, Christmas,
Weddings. He has not been home long enough at any one
time to really understand what has happened to any of
them. I try to help my children, but I have a small inheritance and limited funds."

Katherine and Jeff were raising their children to
get used structure, having respect for themselves and
others, while understanding the value of education, along
with being cautious spenders learning not to overdoing
anything while developing values and financial security.

They felt there was no issue with their thinking,
but they were concerned about Greta taking Mary Jane to
Europe for five weeks. They put pressure on Greta to limit
Mary Jane's spending and not allow her to do things that

normally they would not approve. It was even a stretch for them to allow Mary Jane to fly into Clayton alone for a week before the trip. Katherine let Greta know they were putting a great deal of faith in her at this time. They were happy to know Greta would be at the airport waiting for Mary Jane to arrive.

Greta decided after her senior course was over, she needed to re-focus her attention helping Aunt Rita's daughter, Katherine and her family. Taking Mary Jane to Europe was going to be just the beginning.

Despite Greta's family being small they were close. Greta wanted to see for herself what was needed; that meant being in Chicago and viewing the situation firsthand.

Greta met Mary Jane at the airport and planned on taking her to lunch before addressing anything else. Mary Jane had an idea of her own and she did not want to wait. She did not want to be in Europe looking like a high school student; she wanted to look like a young woman in college. Mary Jane wanted her ponytail gone and hair re-styled and highlighted at once. Greta agreed but wanted lunch first. Reluctantly, Mary Jane, who was hungry, agreed.

Mary Jane gobbled down her lunch feeling she was not going to let too much time in the day go by. While at lunch Greta excused herself and made an appointment at an upscale beauty shop with a certain stylist for Mary Jane. Three hours after lunch Mary Jane's hair was washed, cut, dyed lightly, highlighted with complementary colors and styled. Mary Jane looked quite mature. In fact, Mary Jane looked like a beautiful young woman. Looking in a mirror she was quite pleased at her transformation. She declared the next order of business was to have her ears pierced, and purchase hoop earrings. This was a labor of love for Greta.

Having her ears pierced and buying hooped earrings changed everything for Mary Jane- she was on the way to the look on the outside to complement the way she felt on the inside.

Next, it was time for makeup. It was her belief a young woman going into college and traveling should look attractive and Mary Jane was ready for that next step.

When she mentioned it to Greta said, "We need to take your suitcases out of the car and put them in the house and freshen up we are meeting Ava and Kurt for dinner at 6:15 PM. There will be little time to relax." "But Aunt Greta, with my hair all done and new earrings-the clothes in my suitcases will make me look stupid at dinner -if you get what I mean?" Mary Jane said, with a pouting look on her face. "Aunt Greta, I need some clothes even if they are just for dinner, befitting my look."

With a smile on her face Greta understood. "All right little lady we will stop at Charles Stevens!" Upon arrival they explored the designer's section. An hour later they were on their way to Greta's having bought. two dresses, two pairs of slacks, four matching tops and a sweater coat. "Oh, Aunt Greta, I will look stunning, thank you again." Mary Jane felt ready to enjoy her future as a well-dressed woman. Greta said: "Mary Jane, you will be entering the world of fashions, and you are indeed ready. "Mary Jane just smiled and said, "I love you, Aunt Greta."

They met Ava and Kurt at the "The New Diamonds" Restaurant. Ava was surprised at Mary Jane "You look stunning" she said. Kurt said, "is this the little brides-maid? Boy have you changed."

At the New Diamond restaurant Greta told Mary Jane that an Italian family were the original owners; the restaurant became super successful, and when the owners had a chance to sell and make a large profit, they took it. The new owners more than doubled the place in size; the restaurant now has seating for 150 guests. The new owners offered more of an "Around the World" cuisine.

Their dinner was delicious. Ava enjoyed a Caesar salad, Lamb shanks with potatoes and assorted vegeta-bles; Kurt ordered the Filet with French fries and corn. Mary Jane asked, "Aunt Greta, may I have something—like shrimp or lobster?" Greta found a "Tour of the Sea" dish and suggested she would have an opportunity to taste shrimp, oysters, lobster, and scallops?" "I'm ready, let's go for it." Mary Jane said. Greta ordered a shrimp salad and a cup of onion soup. Mary Jane loved everything but the oysters which Geta finished. Greta said "While these oysters were good, they will be made differently in Paris; and called oysters Rockefeller. You should try them for a great treat.

Visiting, shopping, eating out, and before they realized - their days went by quickly. Ava took Mary Jane to Marshall Fields they met with a makeup consultant, soon Mary Jane was wearing makeup. It was the final touch to make her feel all grown up. While at the store they found a lovely black evening bag, with black three inch heal shoes for evening dinners, and pair of walking and touring shoes for daytime wear.

Next order of business was arranging the suitcases. Outfits needed to be organized. Mary Jane removed a couple of pieces of her old clothes to make space for the new clothes purchased in Chicago. She kept thinking *I am past all this kids' stuff-I am a woman now*!

Chapter 7

A Choice

It was time for Greta to go over rules for travel with Mary Jane:

Greta asked Mary Jane for her undivided attention and began:

"You never leave me, or just walk away.

I must always know where you are.

There really is no reason for you to be without me during the trip, but just in case: you make a "friend" and want to go with that friend I must know:

* Who you are with full name and where they live.
* Where are you going? Store, show, and location
* The time you will be leaving.
* How are you going to go there? Bus, private car
* Whose car, license number.
* If others will be joining, you? Names of joiners
* The time you expect to return to the hotel?
* How are you going to get back? To the hotel?
* Who is the one responsible for taking you out?

We both need to understand the answer to these questions."

It was obvious that Mary Jane listened with half and ear. All the while she was thinking *I will be fine.* As

Greta continued Mary Jane began to cry: "Aunt Greta, I do not need all these rules; I am eighteen years old, a high school graduate, and entering college soon! I am a woman and I know how to behave." Greta was not in a mood for defiance."

She said "Mary Jane you are going to Europe to visit five countries-as a gift. You obviously are and have been treated like an adult the entire time you have been in Clayton. If you want to continue being treated like an adult; you must follow the rules. Traveling abroad is different from living in Chicago. Do not behave rebelliously because that is not acceptable now or at any time we will be traveling. You have never been to any of these countries before-there are different things you need to must understand and be careful about. Am I clear? "Yes" Mary Jane answered. She was stunned at how quickly Greta turned serious.

Greta continued, "There are rules everywhere a person goes, and no one travels especially to a foreign country without understanding the rules. Will I have to remind you of this again?" Greta asked. "No, Aunt Greta but please I am not a child." she said. Greta felt this needed a firm hand and answered her "Mary Jane if the rules are not followed-that will be a signal to me to arrange immediate passage returning home. I can't put it any plainer." Mary Jane never heard Greta be so direct and firm and with a threat to end the trip, she replied, "I am sorry Aunt

Greta I promise to follow the rules." "Thank you, Mary Jane, we need to continue." Greta said, continuing with the rules:

"We never take chances in any foreign country; the laws are different in each country, and rules of behavior are different, along with customs, people and situations are different. I will give you "tips" along the way as we reach each country. We travel to connecting countries by train. I made a list of things to remember for you. But all the following rules leave no room for negotiation. Greta continued,

"As a matter of safety, we do not allow anyone in our hotel room while we are there.

If we are going out, we always meet people in the lobby.

People need to check in with the desk, asking the desk clerk to call us so we could come down to meet them.

Cleaning people are no different; they must wait until you and I are gone before entering the room."

"And...and... and..." Greta continued but despite her efforts Mary Jane appeared to be in her own thoughts and ideas...Mary Jane mind was working overtime—"*I am going to Europe, and with a little luck, I will be free of Aunt Greta! Free to explore...and meet European men! I cannot wait. There may be romance in it for me and who know, I may meet a prince, get married and live in Europe for the rest of my life as a princess!*"

The night before their trip the ladies double checked the labeling on their suitcases and made sure their passports were in a safe place. Each one had a copy of each other's passports as a precaution along as their own passport. Greta explained to Mary Jane, she will receive $50 in cash and $275 in traveler checks as her personal spending money in each country.

Immediately, the idea of having her own money gave Mary Jane a feeling of independence and maturity. She was not just a child traveling with her aunt. Greta had a feeling watching over Mary Jane would require all her attention and focus. Then, Mary Jane asked Greta, "Do I still call you "Aunt Greta? I mean just for the trip?" Greta felt no need to bend any rule, she simply replied, "Of course you still call me Aunt Greta!"

Greta gave Mary Jane her own copy of their complete itinerary with flights, names of the hotels, and "Hub" locations for her purse. This was just in case they were separated for some reason. Ava and Katherine both had a copy of the itinerary.

Ava drove them to the airport and Greta promised to call her whenever possible. Ava stayed and watched the plane take off. As it did, she remembered the times her mother took her to Europe. Ava began traveling with her mother at six years old. She enjoyed all the different countries, getting to meet the people and learning the history of each country (that may have had something to do with why she became a history teacher.) She loved getting to use parts of the native language; those trips were fun and exciting.

But now, she was equally happy to begin her new life as a married woman, in her own home with Kurt as her husband.

Chapter 8

A Family Home

Ava left the airport and drove directly to her "new" house. Kurt was there for questions and checking watching the progress of the renovation. Workers were in every room performing the changes outlined on Ava's list. When Ava arrived there were ladders, lumber, and scrapes of wallpaper covering the floor in the living rooms. The cut plywood in the garage would later be used for raising the attic roof. The entire place was a mess. Ava had to watch where and how she walked. Outside, in front of the house sat a big dumpster to carry all the removed items away.

Kurt felt it would be safer if Ava was not at the construction site. He was confident everything was under his control. But Ava wanted to watch the changes. Ava had her passions:

the kitchen cupboards ordered were Rosewood cherry. She wanted them set-definitely not in the standard way all in a row but by how they were placed in a picture she found in the April, Better Homes and Garden magazine. Next were the closets and storage areas: Ava wanted specific shelving units to put in the closets, and the storage areas. The pantry was to have a double door five shelf unit hung across the entire room. The large pantry was to have six shelves added to the side of the closed cabinet. Each bathroom needed a two shelfed closed cabinet under the sinks, along with four side drawers. A medicine and makeup cabinet would be built into all the bathroom walls next to a full linin closet.

Kurt had all her likes, concerns and wishes written on list. He went over everything with the contractors even though he felt it was ridiculous to put so much into this old house. Ava picked out the counter tops, appliances, light fixtures, kitchen tiles, and six panel doors. The "frosting on the cake" was her decision to add ceiling fans installed in all the bedrooms, dining areas and living room to help with the heating and new cooling air conditioner, she purchased. The ideas for all these items came from pictures in the House and Garden Magazines that Ava loved so well and received every month for years.

Kurt was not impressed with anything, but he did love the solid Bruce cherry hard wood floors they were installing in the entrance way and in the living room.

Kurt did not feel removing a "perfectly good floor" was in order, but he gave in to keep the look of the new floors uniform, he had to admit it looked amazing.

Ava loved shopping, for all the items; her next venture was to purchase a beige rug with a wide deep brown boarder and cream-colored design in the center for the living room. The bedrooms would have wall to wall light toasted beige rugs. The attic roof would be raised; the ceiling height would now be eight feet with sky lights. A full bath on the second and third would be between two guest bedrooms.

Kurt did not like guests, he was not big on all this family stuff. It seemed to him Ava's Mother was always having a get together and people were always traveling to each other's homes much too often. It was difficult for him-he was not social and only lived with his uncle; they had no other family until his uncle married.

Ava wanted the basement completed first with a second kitchen, a half bath, and a large work area dining area. Kurt said the basement would be finished <u>after</u> they moved in; but Ava wanted that completed <u>first.</u> Low and behold it was the first thing tackled and completed. Ava said it made sense-that heavy cooking and canning would be in the basement. The basement was completed, with four men tending to the changes in eight days. The electric and gas installations were ready for the appliances to be delivered and connected later.

Next, on Ava's list was the first-floor master bedroom. It was to be extended out the back of the house on to half of the already existing concrete patio. Then the heat to be extended to cover that addition to the bedroom. To give their first-floor bedroom a touch of romance they also heated and enclosed the other half of the concrete patio. This gave them a private terrace off their bedroom approximately 8x12. It was Kurt's idea. He felt they could sit and sip a little wine and have a private time together. Now their bedroom was 14x16x12x14 with access to a patio 8x12 and two huge closets and a full bath. Part of the area will be for a desk for Kurt.

Moving right along, the wall between the original two bedrooms on the first floor was opened making that bedroom 12x24. For now, this would be a sitting room, or reading room but eventually it would be the baby's room and play area. A full bath was next to the bedroom, the wall opened between the two bedrooms allowed space for a walk-in closet in the master bedroom. While reviewing the plan for the roof, Kurt again approached Ava to leave the inside of the third floor until after they moved in. He did not want to delay leaving from Greta's house.

"I do not want all the mess to finish those rooms after we move in. It is not that difficult to lay the floors, put up walls, and have the bath fixtures put in. We could do the painting later and order the rugs." Ava said. Kurt just said, "Ava gets what Ava wants." And he left the room. The changes being made in the house took it from a five bedroom to a six bedroom; from two full baths to three full baths and now two half baths. Kurt felt it was all so stupid who would believe we were renovating this old house.

The house was structurally sound with an excellent foundation all the money for all this renovation came from Betty and Greta, but Kurt could see no point in even living in a house; a small apartment would have been fine with him. Secretly, Kurt did not enjoy the idea of Ava talking often about having children, he just wanted Ava to himself. He was also concerned that in time Ava would want her mother to live with them. He was totally against that happening. He felt, Greta had too much influence on her daughter.

The house was in walking distance to Greta's. Ava loved having a house that was part of the family for years; "This house is where members of my family were born and grew up. This was the first family homestead." she said. "Just about everyone in my family has lived in it one time or another."

The house gave Ava roots. Ava stayed at the construction site all afternoon and left at 4 PM to cook dinner.

She and Kurt agreed to meet at Greta's house for dinner at 6 PM.

Kurt wanted the renovation completed faster. He asked the foreman to add another crew from 4-10 PM to rush the job.

It would necessitate an additional charge, but he said "Fine" and decided he would deal with that later.

Chapter 9

Mail

Ava arrived at Greta's house just as the mailman was dropping off the mail. He asked her to sign for a registered letter addressed to Greta from a Dr. Cantor in New York.

From the time Ava was a little girl she was taught to date every piece of mail that came in and put it on her mother's desk. In this way, mail would not get lost, and Greta would know the day it was delivered. Ava looked at the envelope at least ten times. She thought: *Mom never mentioned knowing a Dr. Cantor in New York.* Ava was intrigued and curious about the registered letter. Still knowing how both she and her mother felt about privacy Ava did not open the envelope. She placed the envelope face up on the table in the living room until later. The other pieces of mail were dated and placed on her mother's desk. By putting the letter on the table in the living room, she would be reminded to discuss it--next time Greta called.

While preparing dinner Ava walked back and forth from the living room to the kitchen. The letter kept her imagination briming. Ava wanted to know: *Who this doctor was? How did Greta know a doctor in New York City? Was her mother ill? Ava wondered if her mother was ill and put off telling her, because she did not want to spoil Ava's wedding.* Her mind and fears were working overtime.

Cooking dinner her thoughts were on that registered letter. Still, she made Kurt's favorite pork chops marinated in Apple Butter and cider, served with "masked" potatoes and homemade apple sauce. Kurt loved her "masked" potatoes. They were potatoes mashed then blended with a sage stuffing. She made "masked" potatoes either with pork or turkey stuffing. The potatoes and her homemade apple sauce and apple pies were Kurt's favorites.

She made stuffings filled with diced celery, carrots, green peppers, sage sausage and bacon. Over years past, every night, Ava and Greta cooked supper together. The ladies enjoyed mastering cuisines like: French, Italian, Spanish, Puerto Rican and Chinese. Both women were superb cooks.

Greta had a surprise for Ava, she baked an apple spice cake with cinnamon frosting before she left - hid it in the oven-where she was sure Ava would find it. Kurt arrived for dinner at 6 PM starved. Dinner was great and the couple enjoyed the spice cake Greta left with their coffee. They retired to the living room after dinner when Kurt noticed the envelope from a doctor. "What's this? He asked, "is Greta ill?"

"Not to my knowledge" she replied. Ava added; "My mother never mentioned a Dr. Cantor." She sounded a bit concerned. "Should we open it?" Kurt asked. "My mother never liked me to invade her privacy and she always respected mine. I think we had better not. I separated it from the other mail. When Mom calls, I will ask her if she wants me to read it to her."

With a layover in California Greta called home. Ava mentioned work on the house was going to take a four to six weeks longer to complete then originally agreed. Kurt wanted the job completed before Greta returned. He wanted to be out of her house! He even offered the men a bonus if the finished early.

Ava mentioned the letter from Dr. Cantor; Greta assured her she was not ill, but that Dr. Cantor was an old girlfriend from her days of working at the newspaper in New York. Relieved Ava told her mother the letter would be on her desk.

After Greta's telephone call was over Ava dressed and went over to the house wondering how the construction was progressing.

Chapter 10

Surprise

The men were stripping the walls in the attic preparing to expand the third floor into two bedroom and a bath. When that was complete, they planned on removing the roof and heighten the ceiling.

Ava and Kurt were in the living room discussing the carpeting for the second and third floors stairs when they heard the call from the worker yell from the attic "Kurt—Kurt come quick." The man just opened a wall to the sewing room and found it full of new furniture wrapped in plastic.

The two of them raced to the attic. As they arrived, they were flabbergasted to see the room filled with furniture. Grandma Betty had mentioned "Having a special surprise for Ava."

"This must be the surprise Grandma Betty spoke of!" Ava told Kurt. There was a cherry crib, rocking chair, changing table; a sewing machine, a dresser, a three seated sofa and a loveseat with a matching chair, a foot stool, and a beautiful brass set of lamps, covered with plastic. There was enough traditional furniture for the living room and baby's Room with the original sale papers and warranties attached. A white cloth and plastic covered all the beautiful furniture. The furniture in excellent condition.

Betty new they would need furniture to begin living in the house. That room must have been added when Charlie enlarged and divided the attic doubling the size of the sewing room. He kept he the room hidden. There was enough room for anything Betty wanted to add in that room.

Ava wondered *if Greta knew about all the furniture.* It was strange as the house was rented for two years, after Betty died, no one ever needed to get into the sewing room or attic.

Kurt asked the worker to temporarily work in a different area so he and Ava could review the room's contents and decide what to do with the things inside.

The new Westinghouse sewing machine was beautiful with all attachments. Kurt opened what he thought was just a closet and low and behold-there were shelves filled with material and patterns for little girls and women with hundreds of various kinds of thread and sewing equipment.

They decided to put the material into boxes and store them until the house was finished. Kurt picked up one group of materials a book dropped to the floor. It was a journal, and it was dated 1930. He handed it over to Ava. When Kurt picked up another folded piece of material another journal fell. He continued and before their eyes each folded group of material had a journal. There must have been seven journals. The first was from her great grandmother—Mary Jo Wilson. And there were others, Ava became excited "These are secret diaries—Kurt—they are all about my family! Can't you see I now have a history of our family!"

Kurt was not impressed; secret diaries and family history just did not appeal to him. He helped her pack them into boxes with the materials in separate boxes and put them all in her car. Meanwhile he thought *"Why would that old woman put baby furniture in the attic-I do not want a baby for years."*

Ava took the journals and material to her mother's house and put the boxes in her old playroom closet with anticipation of reading the journals later.

The furniture from the attic was moved to their first-floor bedroom; it was finished and safe there for now. Ava added additional covers over every piece of furniture to protect them from dirt. The men continued to remove the old roof, adding the small arch making the height eight feet along with cutting into the ceiling for shy lights. It would look just as Ava saw in a picture about the "Houses of Tomorrow."

The original plan was for the renovation was to be completed in 90 days with eight men, but they were behind.

So, now there were three crews working full days and paid extra on weekends. But things were still not moving as rapidly as expected. One man was out sick another was called in to the Reserves. Two men did not show up all the time. Even materials were delayed being shipped. Consequently, the time has been expanded six weeks additional.

The original plan had them moving in shortly before Greta returned-but as things always do-they were behind schedule.

This made Kurt anxious and frustrated. Kurt did not like living in Greta's house let alone living with Greta. Kurt felt he would be under Greta's thumb without any privacy.

Chapter 11

Time

When their European trip was about over Greta called home; Ava mentioned their house would not be ready for two weeks. Greta said "that is no problem I was going to tell you; I think it would be better if I went to Chicago with Mary Jane. I have a feeling her parents will need me when they see the tattoo Mary Jane had put on her wrist. It is along story honey, but I would like to stay in Chicago for a week and then go on to New York to see my friend and shop. I would like to be gone two more weeks total; would you mind?" Ava said, "Not at all and thank you Mom."

Greta had not planned to extend her time away, but she felt Katherine would need time to adjust to Mary Jane's new clothes, and jewelry. Not to mention the tattoo now on her wrist and the other birthday gift she promised Mary Jane for never breaking the rules.

"Thank you, mom, Ava said, "Enjoy the family and your Dr. friend I will see you two weeks." Greta thought stopping in New York would give her an opportunity her learn why Dr. Cantor sent a registered letter.

Ava asked her to hug everyone for her and let Mary Jane know they would talk later all about her trip as she would call her when they are settled in their new house.

Chapter 12

Their Family

Katherine missed Mary Jane. She was incredibly happy neither one of them were sick, had an accident or injury while in a foreign country. Katherine was a worrier. She was overjoyed Greta did not let Mary Jane fly home alone.

Greta figured Mary Jane's' parents would need help understanding all the clothes purchased while on the trip. She was concerned about Katherine finding the tattoo on her daughters' wrist.

The ladies arrived early in the day. Katherine did see the writing on her daughter's wrist but thought it was just an ink stain that would wash off. Mary Jane had lots of pictures she was excited to show everyone and talk about. She thought the architecture in each country was fabulous. It confused and excited her because now she was not sure if her future would be designing clothes or designing buildings. She was determined to explore and learn which would become her passion.

Greta purchased two extra suitcases to hold the added items Mary Jane brought home. In France, she sent what was left of Mary Jane's old clothes to Chicago by boat. They would arrive in a month. Greta knew she would have to prepare Katherine for the rest of Mary Jane's graduation gift. Over dinner the family listened to stories of the trip from Mary Jane. Greta was aware that Katherine was focused on the tattoo. "What is it?" She asked

Greta knew this would cause an issue. Mary Jane allowed someone to put on the tattoo one evening when she went to a party with a group of young people she met at the hotel while in France. She came back to the room with the numbers already on her wrist. She said, at first, it was something she did just to make the young man happy. She knew it was silly because she was not interested in the boy. She did not realize that removing the numbers would be much of an issue until Greta told her that it needed to be done by a doctor.

Attempting to explain all this to Katherine and Jeff was useless-they kept wanting Mary Jane to "wash it off." Greta explained a couple of times; it could not be washed off and if they would allow Mary Jane to visit her in Clayton again, she would have it removed. Reluctantly they agreed, but Katherine remarked at "How" Greta could "permit such a thing to be painted on her daughter's hand." Katherine would only agree to Mary Jane being gone for four days. "When, she returns those numbers on her wrist need to be gone." Katherine said.

With that issue settled Greta planed the next few days. Greta agreed, while in Europe, to give Mary Jane a new paint job for her bedroom with new drapes and a matching spread all because she followed the rules for travel.

Katherine was shocked that Greta agreed to supply the funds for this adventure of creativity. "You are spoiling her we did not agree to all this. How can we compete with this?" Katherine asked flippantly. "Don't try-just enjoy" Greta answered.

Prior to dinner, Greta called a painting company from the telephone book. They agreed to send a man over within an hour. A man arrived and gave Greta an estimate to paint the bedroom. He suggested two coats and stated he could do the job the next day if the furniture was removed. He wanted Greta and Mary Jane to pick out a color that night; so, he could pick up the paint on his way over in the morning.

The two ladies hailed a cab one hour after supper; Katherine and Jeff began moving things out of the bedroom. They returned home with a sample of the new color, opal white. Katherine said they would finish moving out the bed and mirror in the morning everything else was out. When the painter arrived, the room was empty, and he began his work. It took him four and a half hours to finish two coats. Katherine had to admit-it was lovely, a pearlized soft white was very delicate looking.

Early in the morning, Greta and Mary Jane went to Macy's where Mary Jane picked out sheets, a spread, pillow covers and drapes. Then a canopy bed caught Mary Jane's eye she fell in love with the bed and the design in the wood. She mentioned it was time for her to get rid of the single white bedroom set she slept on since age two, Greta agreed. Macy's did not have the bed in stock but said it could be ordered. Greta wanted Mary Jane to think on it. They asked the salesperson to hold everything, and they would call her before the end of the day to confirm all purchases, the salesperson agreed. Mary Jane left the store deflated.

Their next stop was Montgomery Wards just as the escalator reached the top of the second floor there was a beautiful queen size cherry canopy bed on display. This bed had an arched headboard and footboard it was called a "Sleigh bed." It was stunning. Mary Jane fell in love with it at that moment. It looked regal, and it was quite heavy. Greta had to admit the bed was impressive.

The furniture salesman: a Mr. Smith, told the ladies the bed could be delivered "in two days." Mary Jane was ecstatic but identified one problem: "a new queen cherry bed would look funny mixing it with white furniture. I would need a new dresser, mirror, nightstand, chest on chest and an all-new bed ensemble in queen size."

Greta began laughing and said "So, I suppose. you want it all?" Mary Jane looked pensive and began "Well I do think it would be nice to have; I realize that the entire set would be very expensive." Just then Greta said "Mr. Smith we will take the complete set with a mattress and box spring in Queen. This set is so beautiful, and extremely well built it would last a lifetime. And anyway, this queen bed is befitting for a new college student." At that moment Mr. Smith asked to be excused for a couple of minutes.

Mary Jane was so excited "I can't wait to tell everyone. Thank you, thank you, Aunt Greta. This bed set is so perfect even if I get married it would look nice in my own house." Greta just laughed and said, "I guess you will keep the bed forever then, so it is a great investment in your future as well as a graduation gift." "Yes" Mary Jane answered.

Just then Mr. Smith returned with a shocking surprise. "Well Miss since you are buying the entire set-with a queen mattress and box spring- and it is a graduation gift for your niece-the store manager would like to make this a special gift; instead of a double mirror over the dresser we will be sending a triple mirror- at no extra cost.

That is not all. The manager will be giving you a 15% discount on the complete set without a delivery charge. Congratulations!"

Greta was amazed as she thanked Mr. Smith. He replied, "I remember when my daughter graduated from high school all she wanted was to get rid of that white bed set and have a grown-up set." "I have one more surprise for you-the set can be delivered tomorrow morning around 10:30 AM." Mary Jane was so happy she grabbed Mr. Smith and give him a big hug. The man blushed from ear to ear.

On their way home the ladies returned to Macy's thanked the sales lady, but said they would now need queen bed sheets, blankets, spread, pillow covers and drapes. Mary Jane was going to have an all "new" room tomorrow! But today they needed to explain it all to Katherine.

When the ladies returned home Katherine said that the painter finished. They went in to inspect-it was beautiful. Then they told Katherine this is just in time for the new bedroom furniture that is being delivered tomorrow. Katherine was mortified "Oh my God Greta-what have you done?" Greta replied, "I have made an investment in Mary Jane's future!" Mary Jane and Greta put up the new drapes.

Unfortunately, with all this going on with Mary Jane; attention was lacking for Jeffery Charles, Mary Jane's brother now wanting to be called "JC." Nine-year-old JC was in tears and blurted out: "Does anybody know I am here? I don't want to go to Europe or get a new bed, and I do not need my room painted. I just want boy stuff like the G. I. Joe stuff that is on TV." As he spoke, he walked over to one of the end room tables in the living room and brought over a magazine to show the G. I. games to Greta. At nine-years old that young man did a complete presentation as to why he really "needed the toys." Katherine was upset "JC this is not what you do to people! Leave Aunt Greta alone she had spent enough money on Mary Jane, stop begging for toys."

Greta was impressed with JC, and she listened to everything he said as to why he "Needed the set." When he was through, she kissed him and said it was all right JC, I understand. So, with JC in tow, Greta called and ordered not just the one set the boy mentioned but since he did not have any part of the line, she ordered the complete line of G.I. toys. There was over 200 pieces with all the sets including: including: men, training buildings, barracks, airplanes, guns, and tanks. For an extra cost, the complete line would be delivered overnight - by noon, the next day. JC was so excited he hugged and kissed Greta. When Katherine heard Greta on the telephone, she tied to get her attention to stop her from ordering; but when Greta gave the man on the telephone her credit card, Katherine just left the room saying it was "No use to try to and stop Greta."

Chapter 13

Much to Do

Rita was invited to dinner one evening, previously she mentioned to Greta the financial strain Katherine and her husband were in. Rita mentioned Katherine and Jeff had applied for a loan against the house to bring their bills up to date and pay the first quarter for Mary Jane's college. Earlier Greta saw Rita hand an envelope to Katherine. When dinner was over: Greta and Rita went for a walk. Greta asked Rita about the envelop Rita said she "I gave Katherine had a few hundred dollars to help them accumulate the money needed for the processing fee on the loan application."

After Rita left, Greta spoke with Katherine and Jeff. She asked questions that embarrassed them. They could not believe Rita mentioned anything; but Katherine said "When we purchased this house two years ago, we knew it needed work and the appliances were old. When Jeff's company merged it took time for him to locate a new job. Jeff took a small cut in pay when he was hired by Cambridge, Inc; but this job was just what he was looking to find. He has great promise of upward movement in the future if he sticks it out." Katherine said, "I am still at my part time job; when Jeffery Charles gets a little older, I plan on getting a full-time position." Katherine did not want to belabor the issues "Greta we will be fine it is just a small set back; and everything we need will come in time." And with that she said "good night and went to bed.

Greta understood and she was resolved to do something to help.

From the telephone in the kitchen, Greta dialed the Montgomery Ward 24-hour Catalogue number. The gentleman on the phone was most helpful. Greta mentioned she wanted "Santa to come to her cousin's home early this year," the man understood what she wanted to do. He told her they had a warehouse only five miles from Katherine's house. Greta named each one of the appliances she wanted. The man verified that all those appliances were in their warehouse in LaGrange Park.

Greta ordered a Maytag washer and dryer, a GE dishwasher, an incinerator garbage disposal, Frigidaire 36-inch gas five burner oven and range, two Kenmore 30-inch televisions, a Kenmore stand up 22 cubic foot stand up freezer, a 25 cubic foot refrigerator. The last item was a 1200/watt microwave. The microwave was not available it would take two weeks before delivery. Microwaves were new and not easily available. Greta agreed no microwave would be in the order; but a new four slice toaster would take its place with an electric coffee pot.

Greta agreed to the extra fees for the eight men to come an install all appliances the next day. The man returned with the confirmation number from her credit card and a surprise. While processing the order, his manager reviewed all the appliances being bought and decided to waive the delivery charges on all the items bought. Greta felt quite proud of herself, she made two young people incredibly happy. Now it was time to let Santa do his thing and watch the excitement.

The gentleman said everything would arrive at the house between noon-1:30 M and installation would be completed by 5:45-6:30 PM.

The next morning, Greta went out before breakfast leaving Katherine a note. She went to the Central Loan Bank where Rita said Katherine had a mortgage and an application for a loan. The current mortgage balance was $49,512. but the late fees were an added $3,500. She negotiated with the bank officer by agreeing to pay off the entire loan without fees; and then setting up two trust accounts in their trust department with long term Certificates of Deposit for both Mary Jane and Jeffery Charles that would be sufficient to pay all their college costs. The bank manager agreed and when the wire transfer of funds was complete a satisfaction of mortgage was signed; it would be recorded later the next day by the bank attorney. The officer gave Greta two photocopies one for Katherine and Jeff and one for her files.

All this banking took three hours, Greta was hungry. She stopped at the Stengel's Restaurant and ordered lunch. On her way to lunch she found a telephone booth and called an old friend at Russell's Buick Dealers. Greta knew the owner of the dealership and wondered if he remembered her. The owner was impressed at her business savvy. He liked Greta and twenty years ago had even tried to date her. He understood what she was trying to do and told her "You want two cars for dealer's cost, delivered to the house, the next morning; with one being white and the other cobalt blue, am I correct?" Well, it just so happens they were on my lot. A salesperson will be there, with the cars delivered, to complete the paperwork at 11 AM. After her lunch, Greta agreed to stop by the dealership and give them her check.

Greta arrived back at the house at 12:50 PM the new appliances arrived 1PM. She just made it in as Katherine was cleaning when the doorbell rang. Katherine said they were at the wrong house-then Greta stepped in greeted the men telling them they were at the right house and to please come in. All eight of the men came in to set up the new appliances and televisions. At 5:55 PM all the appliances were installed. There were three men in the kitchen, two in the laundry and the last three setting up TV's one in the living room, one in the family room and hooking up the old television set in Katherine and Jeff's bedroom. All new appliances completed and per her agreement all appliances: freezer. oven and range, refrigerator, washer and dryer, were hooked up in the basement. Katherine's head was spinning and when Jeff walked in, he could not believe what was happening.

When the men were leaving, Greta rallied the children, Jeff and Katherine and called Rita asking her to be ready in Twenty-five minutes as they would pick her up and head out to dinner at "Grandma's Home Cooking Family Restaurant."

The place was small with seating for only ninety people, but it was clean, neat and the food was excellent and reasonably priced. Everything was served family style with large plates placed on the table. Greta had the restaurant reviewed five times for the paper because the food was so good. She ordered the family specialty of the house, which consisted of two kinds of potatoes: French fries and mashed, a roast pork platter with stuffing, fried chicken and meatloaf. The meal was served with corn on the cob, cooked carrots, green beans, and apple pie for dessert with complementary coffee or milk for the little ones.

When Katherine saw the cost per person for this special, she tried to say it would be too much-but when the food arrived it was all delicious and no one really wins when Greta is around.

With homemade apple and a cherry pie ordered for dessert, with ice cream everyone ate as much as they could. Whatever food was left on the table, they were allowed a take home. Katherine said they had enough food for another dinner. But when she saw the bill, she told the kids this was a "Once in a lifetime treat!"

It was a beautiful evening; everyone enjoyed their special meal. Katherine and Jeff thanked Greta a dozen times for their new appliances and televisions. Rita thanked Greta "I know Carl would have helped but it..." Greta interrupted, "I was happy to have the opportunity do it-I think it all went well-don't you? Rita what is money for if not to help family in need." "Yes, and you did it beautifully Greta, thank you." said Rita.

The next morning was Saturday, and everyone was home watching the television. At 11 AM the doorbell rang. A salesperson from Russell's was at the door with all the paperwork to be signed by both Jeff and Katherine for their new cars. Jeff felt there must be a mistake-but Greta interrupted and assured him it was "No mistake Jeff, I bought two cars yesterday and they will belong to you and Katherine as soon as you sign the papers. Jeffery and Katherine were stunned and in tears- "Two new cars Greta and after all you have done for the children and for us in the house —how could we ever thank you..."

Greta interrupted and said, "How long would you two be able to handle one five-year old car. It was my pleasure to help. The best use of money is to help family, and I love all of you very much." As soon as the papers were signed the family went out to inspect the cars. Rita just arrived and was stunned at Greta's kindness. Greta suggested "The two cars are the same except the white one is for Katherine because she loves white; Jeff are you ok with the navy blue-someone once told me that was your favorite color?" "The colors are perfect Greta, and you remembered our likes perfectly," said Jeff. "I was thinking, since you two each have your own car, is it possible your old car might be given to Mary Jane for school? Busses are tough in the winter."

Mary Jane was ecstatic hearing Aunt Greta's suggestion. Her parents agreed it would save her, especially in the winter. Hugs and Kisses were now shared. Greta told Jeff there is a check in the envelope from her to him that should cover the cost of insurance on all three cars for two years. "By then your situation should be in good shape." Jeff thanked her again and said that they appreciated all her gifts. With everyone back inside the house and at the table Greta pulled out four envelopes: "Jeff, these are papers from your bank-your mortgage has been paid in full; the papers are being recorded today." "Oh my God Greta, I cannot believe you did that-but how OMG you're amazing …" Greta interrupted "Mary Jane you now have a trust fund your college, it is paid in full with extra funds available for gas and repairs on the car;" she continued. "JC my man you also have a trust fund, and your college will also be paid in full. I love you all very much!" Everyone rallied around Greta, tears were flowing. Rita was stunned as she sat and listened to how all Katherine and Jeffery's issues have been whisked away in just days of Greta being there for a visit—*she was so good to everyone*. Rita thought.

Rita reminded Greta of the time "We need leave for our lunch reservations.," Greta noticed how happy the faces of her cousin, and her family looked. Everyone was in tears so incredibly grateful. Greta's heart felt good— she knew this was the right thing to have done for them. Their future will be now much brighter and happier.

Greta planned a small side trip to New York City. She wanted to see old friends and especially Dr. Cantor. She was interested in why Dr. Cantor sent her a registered letter. The next day Rita was taking Greta to lunch, and then would drive her to the airport.

In the car Rita said "Greta, you have done so much for Katherine and her family, thank you. They will have a better future and a life not having to worry about anything lest of all college for their kids. I wish there was something we could do for you and Ava." "There is nothing I need Rita—except for you to travel to Clayton with Mary Jane next week when she comes to remove the tattoo. I would like you to ask Katherine if Mary Jane could stay a week instead of just four days. That would give Ava and Kurt a chance to see you and you could visit and seeing the renovation on the house. And us girls could be commiserating on out next trip together. We could all have a wonderful time. What do you say, Rita?"

"Oh Greta, I love that idea, it is a done deal. I will bring Mary Jane there in next week and explain to Katherine that we need a week. I'll call you and tell you what time our plain arrives." "Great said Greta as she opened her purse, here are two tickets to Clayton for next Thursday one for you and one for Mary Jane." Rita was stunned "Greta you are terrific-we will be there and thank you again. "No problem I love you all very much.

Then Greta asked, "Aunt Rita, what is happening with Joseph Carl?" "Well Greta, it isn't good. You know his wife is a nurse well lately she has been taking extra shifts. Joseph Carl is not sure why, but she does love her job. We will have to wait to understand what is happening. The boys are doing great in school, both are in sports. I heard from Shana last night David Junior has a cold, but the rest of the children are doing great. Connie sends her love and Pasquale asked for you to visit them when you are in New York." Greta's flight to New York was uneventful except landing in La Guardia a bit late.

Chapter 14

New York

After checking in at her hotel, Greta's called Dr. Cantor's office. It had been years since the two of them had seen each other and, knowing there was a registered letter in Clayton waiting, Greta wanted to learn why, what happened?

Dr. Cantor married ten years earlier her married name was "Marsh;" professionally she continued using Dr. Cantor.

The doctor's receptionist said the doctor was with a patient. Greta left her name, the hotel she was staying at, her room number and asked for the doctor to return her call.

Two hours later she received a call from Dr. Cantor. They exchanged pleasantries and decided to meet for dinner at 6PM n the hotel lobby and then proceed to the hotel restaurant. Dr. Cantor mentioned her father would be joining them for dinner.

Greta's curiosity was now heightened; wondering if there was something in Slade's "will" she forgot. "*I wonder why Dr. Cantor's father, Slade's attorney, is joining us?*" she thought.

The ladies met in the lobby of the hotel and proceeded to the restaurant, just sat down at a quiet table, Mr. Cantor walked in and joined them. Greta had forgotten how handsome Mr. Cantor was-at seventy-four years old, the man kept his looks, with silver hair topping his sturdy 6-foot 2-inch-tall frame; and at about 250 pounds he looked perfectly attractive. They ordered drinks and dinner. Then they each caught up on the happenings in their lives. Finally, Mr. Cantor mentioned he wanted to discuss business.

He began, "Greta, there is a buyer for the medical building and the price offered of 1.3 million dollars, it is line with the current market value. Since Slade West's will left the ownership of the building to Ava, once she reached the age of twenty-two, I think this needs to be discussed with her."

Greta agreed stating "Ava, as you recall, still has no knowledge of her father's estate or her inheritance." Greta asked the name of the purchaser and was surprised to learn it was Dr. Cantor and Michelle Cantor, Mr. Cantor's ex-wife and Dr. Cantor's mother.

"I do not understand" Greta said. He continued, "Michelle has worked as Lisa's nurse for the last eighteen years. They feel that both she and Lisa cared for the building all these years and they should own it. Michelle and I divorced twelve years ago but we are still partners looking out for our daughter. Michelle and Lisa live together, with Lisa's three children, in an apartment. Lisa's husband gambled away her money and she had to sell their home to pay his gambling debts. She is close to not having any money. Besides her lucrative practice and working six days a week owning the building would help her get back on her feet."

To prepare for her discussion with Ava about the sale of the building and her estate; Greta as trustee for Ava, asked for three appraisals from reputable real estate brokers in the area to show the fairness of the offering price; an updated current annual statement showing all rents, leases and repairs. She said, when these things were available and after seeing the condition of the building; she would have everything needed either decide on the sale or discuss the sale with Ava. Mr. Cantor said, "no problem" and gave her the name and telephone number of their accountant. He assured her everything would be ready by the end of the week for her review. Dinner was over and Mr. Cantor paid the bill.

Chapter 15

Getting Ready

Greta called Ava and told her she was staying in New York a bit longer to take in a few plays and shop. Over the next three days Greta visited the clinic and spoke with the tenants. The building was kept up beautifully and the additions put on two years earlier were artistically completed. The building did not look thirty years old. The grounds were filled with flowers and greenery. The entire entrance lobby had lovely fresh greenery.

The appraisals came in with four comparable buildings in an area closer to the Magnificent Mile worth between 1.4-1.7 million dollars since compliance to the laws for handicap were completed. Competitive sales in the area closer to the building averaged 1.2-1.4 million.

A letter from the city confirmed, two years ago the building complied with the laws for handicap on; all entrances and exits, along with all-bathrooms having safety features. The costs of such compliances were accounted for in the trust annual statements for Ava.

The accountant statement identified that the building has been fully rented with rents increasing according to market. The trust had more than needed to cover the expenses and changes for the handicap.

As per Slade West's will, the net rents for the last twenty-one years were placed in a trust account for Ava. It was clear to Greta that Dr. Cantor, and her mother deserved to own the building.

Since Greta was the trustee for Ava, she chose to give Dr. Cantor and her mother an acceptance their offer of $1.35 million to purchase the medical building. Mr. Cantor, Michell Cantor and Dr. Cantor agreed to meet with Greta in the hotel restaurant when she agreed to the sale; Mr. Cantor would be giving her the papers to sign.

Since Mr. Cantor would be the attorney representing his wife and daughter; he gave Greta the name of four reputable Real Estate attorney's she could use to close the transaction for her and Ava. Greta knew one of them very well. She dated him years ago and they were friends.

A fifteen-year private mortgage was needed to complete the purchase after a $50,000 down payment was made. In the offer, it was a requested that the mortgage be held at the going interest rate, as an addition to Ava's trust. Greta agreed "It was like money in the bank for Ava's future." Mr. Cantor said he would contact her attorney to complete the paperwork for the mortgage and prepare the closing.

Mr. Cantor told Greta, he would be in Clayton soon; and would like to meet Greta for dinner. Greta agreed. He suggested: "Greta I believe we should discuss the sale of the medical building with Ava. It would be a good time to discuss the terms of her father's will. I could help her understand it all better than just handing her copy of the will. With her twenty-second birthday close and now being married I feel confident she will have questions."

Greta reminded Mr. Cantor "There is one thing that cannot be discussed with Ava." Mr. Cantor said, "I assure you Greta it will never be mentioned, the letters accepting responsibility from Slade for the rape have been destroyed per your request after Ava was born."

Greta said, "I will be happy to set up the dinner, give me a call when you are arriving in Clayton, and I will set it up with Ava."

She thanked everyone and, extending her regrets to Lisa for enduring a rough ten years during her marriage.

They all hugged, and Greta left. When Greta left the restaurant, *she wondered how she was going to tell Ava about her trust fund. She thought about preparing Ava before the dinner-but in a second dismissed the thought.*

I know my daughter she will be grateful for all my effort and work that I put into managing the estate while giving her an exposure to the world, sound values and a great, loving and close upbringing.

Chapter 16

It's Time

"Home" in the United State Greta realized that traveling, wet her desire to write about the world's greatest places to visit. This idea would help her to get back into the life she once loved. She was not sure if it would be a book or a professional column, but she leaned to joining a travel television show and establishing a crew to travel with her.

She had a passing thought that it would be neat if Rita joined her on three of these trips. After all Rita was retired, her children were married; and Carl travels constantly for his burn cream; and Shana and Rita are close.

Greta would never consider the thought of feeling lonely by herself. The last twenty-one years with Ava always at her side she was never lonely but now with Ava married...

Ava told Greta the renovation on their house would be completed in that week. She said that they had already begun moving things into the house. Greta made reservations to return to Clayton two days before the truck came for the remainder of Ava's things. She left New York knowing that Ava and Kurt were still living in her home. She called Ava and asked her if she was able to pick her up at the airport. Ava agreed.

Chapter 17

Betty

Betty knew renovating the house would take cash; she also knew Ava's love of traditional furniture. She wanted to make the move easier. As a wedding gift Betty left Ava $30,000 in cash from her will. Betty loved Ava and her great granddaughter loved her dearly. Betty's only regret was not lasting in this world long enough to be at Ava's wedding. Betty passed away with three years before the wedding.

Betty's heart had been broken over the stress of Kevin's behavior, toward her. His unrelatability, rudeness and indifference destroyed hope for love. closeness and true companionship.

Working at the church there was a gentleman-widowed five years ago earlier who often asked her to go to coffee. While he was a pleasant sort, Betty wanted Kevin; the man she gave her heart to, and no one could replace him. She never went to coffee with the man but thanked him. His greeting was always "Keep the faith sunshine." Betty just smiled.

The Christmas Kevin gave her the brushoff and disregarded her kindness and consideration of taking two buses to visit him- in the cold of winter was the end for Betty. He took her gift and gave it to a worker at the residence, then he put the cookies she made specially for him on the table for all to eat. He then went to another woman and sat near her laughing.

She never returned to see him after that happened. She cried for a month. When the administrator of the senior center called and told her that Kevin passed away in his sleep, Betty took care of the arrangements for his funeral. She did everything.

In Kevin's will he left Betty a sizeable amount of cash, and as his widow, her social security was increased.

He left Rita the same amount. All the rest of his funds went to Michael and Nora.

Betty was hard pressed to bury Kevin at the place where the two of them were originally to be buried; instead, she buried him as close to Mary Jo as possible. Kevin originally purchased two plots when Mary Jo died but he sold the second one when he married Betty.

Betty sold the site where the two of them where to be buried. "He did not trust or want me in life why should I be near him in death." She wrote in her will to her executive Michael. Instead, she purchased plot for herself near her mother.

Betty never squandered money in fact she never used all the money Kevin or Charlie left her when they passed away. It was used to keep up the house or to invest with the intention of giving money to Michael and Nora, Greta and Ava.

Betty loved Kevin, nothing and no one could ever fill her heart with joy again. It was a shame, but no one could change Kevin's thinking-he had his opinion and made his decision, holding on to it was his downfall and hers. He wasted twenty-five years of love from a truly devoted woman.

Knowing that Betty left the house to Ava, Michael and Nora moved out of the house into an apartment after Betty's death. In this way Ava could rent the house. This was all planned. Betty gave them the option of staying in the house until they died but they wanted to return to an apartment.

Chapter 18

Ava & Kurt's Wedding

Greta gave the kids a beautiful wedding. Ava never expected to receive a wedding gift from Greta. But Greta surprised them and along with the honeymoon gave them $30,000 in cash.

Not only did Kurt pay for nothing, but his uncle also never came to the wedding or sent a card. There were 150 guests at the wedding held at the "It's Now" Ball Room just outside of Clayton. most were friends of Ava, Greta and family. The weather was in the low 70's and sunny for the wedding. Ava's dress was her own design, not your typical wedding dress. Instead, it was more of an evening gown in a light crochet off white knit with a round dipped front and three-quarter sleeves. The dress was fit to her body beautifully as it went to the floor. The bride wore a pill-box hat with a hair top veil and off-white pumps. It was beautiful. Kelly Mc Caffery was maid of honor. She was a friend of Ava from high school. She designed and made her dress. It was also a light crochet cobalt blue knit with a "V" neck and three-quarter sleeves, "A" lined, to flatter her figure.

Mary Jane was the second bridesmaid. She was dressed in a powder blue empire waist dress pencil dress with a "V" neck, fitted to her with a braid around the "V" neck, three-quarter sleeves and the empire design.

The bridesmaids each carried three orchards; Ava's carried a one orchard with three lilies in her bouquet. Greta wore a weaved blue and white knit suit. With three quarter sleeves topped off with a powder blue blouse, with a high collar and a beautiful pin from Betty.

Ava's dress was different; it was so weaved that it almost looked like hearts were in the weave. Both mother and daughter knew that this was it; they would no longer be living together. Ava, now a married woman and would soon be living in her own home. It was going to be hard for both of them- almost twenty-two years together, traveled together, shopped together, at times slept together, cooked together and loved life together--they were never apart.

When the house was finished Kurt hired a moving company to move everything from Ava's room and playroom including the boxes of journals to the new house. Items were placed in the in the basement until Ava had a chance to organize the house. Ava told Greta about the sewing room, the furniture, but not about the journals. In fact, she forgot about them until one night.

Chapter 19

Boxes

The boxes were labeled, Ava went down the basement to show to the mover where everything in the basement was to be put. Everything that did not fit upstairs or was not labeled was stacked in a corner in the finished basement. Ava forgot what was inside many of the boxes and she was unable to tell the contents by the labeling. She opened five boxes and began putting items away. The first group of boxes were for their bedroom and Kurt's office area.

Then she noticed a tag and remembered these were the journals found in the attic. One by one Ava brought those boxes up to the first-floor second bedroom. This room was temporarily made into a guest room. The room had a large walk-in closet where Ava placed all the boxes. Being most curious about the first box Labeled "Mary Jo." She sat down on a chair and decided to read "just a little."

On the first page was written:

"This writing belongs to Mary Jo Wilson"

"It is now May 1st. Kevin and I both work two jobs. It is not easy for us. We are saving everything we make cause r dream is to own a house. We want a home of r own cause neither of r families has 1 r families pay rent.

Kevin says we are goanna own a house one day soon cause it is r dream.

I have another dream - a baby but Kevin says, "we cannot afford a baby for a long while." He is rite. I got this riting book from Mrs. Arcana. She says it will be good for me to rite words. I do not understand why but I like riting. She is helping me with my spelling, so my words are good.

We moved often we eat soup and bologna all the time. I wish for something else but if I mention it to Kevin, he will feel hurt. He got a third job. I do not know how he does it. He says we are moving into his friend's place. I have not seen it, but Kevin says it is bigger and it has a toilet right in the place no more peeing in an empty coffee can like in the place we are staying.

Wow-Kevin did good this place has a sink and a two-burner gas stove with a table. If we did not have to work so many jobs-we might like being here. It costs more than over the garage, but Kevin made a deal with that property owner.

Mrs. Arcana gave me spelling books to read. She thinks I am smart and need to just read how to rite and spell better, I told her I need to find time.

Here we are again moving. Kevin said it was time to move and we moved. We are both working-three jobs.

We want a house but all we do is work-and move there is no time for anything else. I am learning how to spell every day. It is helping because I also need to spell correctly at the restaurant. There will be little money left after we pay this new rent; we did a budget.

I have been reading the books from Mrs. Arcana and working on my spelling and writing. I really want to get a high school diploma. If I get a real diploma, I could get a more better paying job and only work one job. Mrs. Arcana told me I did the last sentence wrong-it should have been I could get a better paying job. Mrs. Arcana says that I have made great strides in my writing, spelling, and thinking. I am happy about that and so is Kevin.

Kevin says all our hard work will pay off-but my feet hurt, and I cannot tell him, or he will feel bad. Mrs. Arcana says she will still work with me even if we move. I am so happy because she used to be a teacher in a real school.

Well-you guessed it we are moving again to a nice warm cottage.

Well, I had no time to write for a year. We are still in the cottage, but we are moving again. One day we will move into a house then I will find time to write more.

My writing and spelling have increased. I even read novels that I get from Mrs. Spring. She used to be a teacher as well.

Chapter 20

Dreams Can Come True

Guess what-we are moving again this time to our own house. Kevin's friend Donald wanted to move to a warm climate. He is selling us his house; he and his wife are moving to California.

Kevin says it will be a bit further for us to get to work, but it will be our house. He went to the bank and talked with those people and then went to Mrs. Dorm's legal man. When pay Donald and the bank and have the insurance then the house will be ours.

It took us many times back and forth to finish bringing our belongings to the house we carried our stuff here in the rain. We gave Donald cash and signed papers. We did it all and guess what----we moved into the house.

Kevin says we must pay Donald $20 per month and then pay the bank and the insurance man. We need to pay all that before it is legally all ours even though we live in it. I am worried, this house costs a lot of money. Our money is almost gone. When I try to talk with Kevin about my fearing, we would lose the house he just says, "We will have this house forever" and to "just trust him." I love him but I am still crying.

Mrs. Arcana told me to date my writing if I remember.

September 30

We are in luck a friend of Kevin's is our insurance agent. his name is Mark Row and Karena is his wife. We are all becoming friends. Kevin will work for Mark and sell insurance together. He will be in the professional category. Mark is going to be Kevin's teacher and pay Kevin to learn the business. While Kevin is learning insurance Karena is helping me look pretty and cook French. I know how to cook Italian because I learned from Mrs. T's mother.

April 9

Well Kevin passed the insurance exam and we celebrated at the Swiss Chalet restaurant. I love the food. Kevin gave up his night job of cleaning. He only wants to sell insurance. I am still working with Mr. and Mrs. T. at Diamonds; they love me, and I love them. Well, we paid all our bills again this month.

August 9

My mom is sick. My father stopped by the house and told me to visit her. I told him I would on my day off. I wonder why she was sick—maybe she is tired of working; his drinking, spending her money and him hitting her in the stomach? Who knows what it is?

He always hits her in the stomach when he is drunk-he used to say, "no one would ever believe her because he does not leave any marks on her." He hit her hard -the day she was mad at him, for what he did to me in my bedroom. I can never tell Kevin. My mom will never tell anyone because my mom said if she told the police what my father did to me - my father would go to jail. I think my dad is afraid of Kevin so he will not tell him what he did. My mom was sick. I am going to visit her today.

Oh boy, my mom is bad sick, she stayed in bed. Her color is bad, she has pain in her stomach. There is no money for a doctor. My father called the mid wife Mrs. Arcana, and she came. She told my dad my mom is going to die soon. I said that sounds crazy Mom is only 47 years old. Mrs. Arcana does not know what made mom so sick, but she is sure my mom is going to die soon.

Well, I think Mrs. Arcana must have special power because my mom died. My father came and asked for money to bury her. I spoke with Kevin; he will pay all the bills. I love that man so much I will do anything for him. Kevin is a good man we know my dad would never pay us any money. My husband paid all $89 for casket and planting her. My mom is paid up. This will put us bahind but I love Kevin more every day.

Chapter 21

Learning

January 4

It has been a long time since I wrote in this book. We paid the cemetery off. We went to the Goodwill and spent almost $3.00 on thread, needles, buttons and a tape measure-I have a big box of all this, it came with a book on how to sew things. Kevin bought paint brushes and a measuring box tape. We tell people I will sew buttons, and Kevin sells insurance.

He will paint our house when we get more money. I made $1.00 this week on buttons. I sew them for ten cents each. Kevin painted a small sign for Mr. Galvano, and he got paid $2.25.

Diamonds has become more re-refined since it was redecorated, and we are offer high priced meals. I am learning how to speak better, write neater, and spell better. I have learned how to cook every meal we offer along with the Italian sauce. I am going to do both the cooking and being a server in the restaurant. I am learning how to write down the orders for the cook so she could read them in a sort of shorthand way.

Angie devised a system since our dinners are numbered all I need to write down is the number of the meal from the menu and any specific changes the customer wants. It is working. All the servers have been learning the system from Mrs. Spring. The restaurant is getting so fancy. Servers must wear black pants and white tops. Mr. T pays for the clothes we wear. No one likes the dress he picked so we just wear the pants and top. I am even learning a little Italian.

Mrs. Spring says I am her star student. Both my spelling and writing have improved. I am finished learning how to cook everything in the restaurant. Mrs. T's mother was sick one day and went home-I cooked all the orders. Mrs. T said everything was "terrific." Guess what, I got a raise.

Six months have passed since that last entry. I am still doing much of the cooking. I have been given three raises on the days I only cook. I have come a long way. I brought home $55 per week for each of the last three weeks. I cooked for five days and then Mrs. T cooked for the last two days. Next week the restaurant will have two parties and I will cook for both. I will get a bonus of double my pay, because the people at each party will take the whole restaurant. It will be a lot of cooking and planning. Mrs. T helps because her mother is not well, and she does not come into the restaurant often.

Well, the first party was just over—do you know what -a man from that party did—he asked to see the cook. When I came out of the kitchen, he handed me a

$20 bill and said this "is the best Italian food I have had in years." Mrs. T said I could keep the money. Kevin and I used that money and both weeks of my pay to finally pay off Donald. Now all we must worry about is the bank and the cost monthly for homeowners' insurance.

Chapter 22

Friends

Well, these last two months have been so busy that I forgot all about the high school test. This house is really a dream come true. When we moved to our house, I spent three days just washing the floors and cleaning the bathroom and the basement. Kevin said the kitchen was terribly sticky and he used a solution that a neighbor brought over to clean. The solution smelled bad, but it worked. Cleaning the house is harder work than cooking in the restaurant. There are still things that needing fixing in the house we will do them when we get the money, right now since I am making good money cooking, we will concentrate on paying the bank. We love owning our home!

A neighbor brought over homemade banana bread. She left a paper with her name and telephone number just in case we need anything. The banana bread was delicious, and she offered to bring over the recipe and teach me how to make it.

Another neighbor came over with fresh vegetables from her garden. I don't quite remember her name, but we were given two zucchinis, 30 green beans, four tomatoes and three large green peppers. I cannot wait to cook and eat them. I will make eggs first cooking them with green peppers for breakfast tomorrow. Kevin will get pick up olive oil on his way home. I like olive

Oil to cook with; the food tastes great with it.

Owning a house makes me comfortable inside. Kevin likes working for Mark and I like his wife, Karena. They take us out to a new restaurant occasionally. I will go to a special thrift shop before the next dinner. The shop I want to go has everything and if you are nice to the lady, she even makes things cheaper.

Kevin did not get new clothes, but I bought a dress, and it was very pretty. Kevin said I looked nice; I wore the makeup Karena taught me to use.

Kevin said he is making enough money-to take us to another level. Not sure what that means. I do not have the right clothes to go to a place like the one Mark's wife likes to eat at. She always looks beautiful. I am not pretty. I cannot even pronounce the name of the restaurant we went to-but Mark told us to order whatever we wanted. Kevin told me not to add more than 50 cents over what-ever the cost of Mark's or his wife's meal was to the cost of my meal. We each ordered what was ordered by Mark or his wife. After we finished Karena ordered apple pie and coffee for everyone. The piece was so big Kevin and I split one so we could take the other one home for later.

We do not drink coffee often, we were up half the night, but it was worth it. Karena says she has "tons of cherries in her yard." She insisted they would come over on Saturday and we will bake a cherry pie. She came with three bags of stuff: two were all foods and pie tins, one had a big bag of coffee and a coffee pot. There was a third bag and she said that would be for later. Together we made three pies and coffee. She said she would take one pie home-but we will have two in our refrigerator.

Kevin and Mark just talk—they went for a walk to talk—Mark said there was stuff at their house they are not using, and Karena and he will bring the items over on Saturday to help us decorate our house—a dream come true.

Before the men came back, Karena opened the third bag. There was a white dress-up blouse in it and a black skirt with a slip. She told me that we were about the same size and when I tried the things on, they all fit. They had tags on them all from a store—the items were new! She told me not to tell Kevin and to wait until we were all going out and just wear the clothes to see what he would say. I hid the clothes under the bed. I will save them for a special time. Karena says never wear strips and flowers together they do not go together well. I will use soft colors-because they go nicely with my hair but no red.

I don't let anyone see this book but me and I know when I write. But I guess I will remember to put the month in occasionally.

Chapter 23

A Baby

October

Mrs. Arcana came into the restaurant and said my father has a girlfriend. I really do not like my father-he is a bad. He is getting married again and moving to Ohio. All my siblings left home. I would like to see my brothers and sister one day. I don't care about my dad.

December 11,

I have been feeling tired. I missed three days at work. Karena says I need a doctor, but we do not have one or the money to go to one.

On December 15, we are supposed to go to Mark and Karena's for dinner-but I still feel sick. I made an apple pie and could not eat it. I hope I do not have what Mom had because she died. Kevin ate a tomato sandwich for dinner tonight and we just sat and played rummy. My stomach is constantly wanting me not to eat.

December 24

6 PM Karena and Mark came over. They brought-a small Christmas tree with lights on it and popcorn strung all over it.

It was beautiful. Karena bought over a new red towel to put around the bottom of the tree. They brought packages all wrapped pretty. I got a new scarf and a pair of earrings; Kevin got a tie and a belt.

We both felt bad because we did not have gifts for them. I never shop for gifts-Kevin never gave me a present and I never gave him one. All our money goes to pay down the mortgage -just like the banker lady said. But they loved the apple pie and coffee, I sent home a pie just for them.

On Christmas Karena sent over a pork dish with stuffing. On Christmas her parents and sister are going over their house for dinner. We loved the pork, and the stuffing was delicious. Two hour later the whole thing came up. Kevin is worried and he wants me to see a doctor.

Guess what? Karena took me to her doctor--I AM PREGNANT! I am so happy. I will tell Kevin in a couple of days but for now just Karena and I know. There were things the doctor needed to do-it was a shock, but he was a doctor! The doctor thinks the baby will come sometime the end of May because I was pregnant and did not know it.

I made a special dinner and even put candles on the table. Kevin came home and was worried about the tests I took, and my being so sick. But when I told him about a baby, he was happy. I asked him if I could stay home when the baby is born. I know we need the money. How can someone be happy and sad at the same time? He said it would be ok.

March 15,

I am tired. I still throw up every now and then. I hope the baby is ok. I sleep when I get home from work and a couple of days ago, I forgot to cook supper. I made soup the day before. Food does not make me hungry-at the restaurant sometimes I cannot even bring a plate to a table without getting sick. Mr. T says I will have to quit soon. They are such wonderful people. I now can cook Italian and French.

I get salad and fruit from the restaurant but what I like most is the spaghetti. Karena is going to teach me how to keep the books for Kevin and make his appointments.

April 2

The vomiting has not stopped. Kevin is losing patience with me because he does not understand why I am getting so fat. I am borrowing his shirts and when he wants a T-shirt I have it on. I think we need to buy more clothes for him but that will have to wait until sometime around Christmas.

Since, I told Mrs. Arcana about the baby moving all the time she has been helpful and kind. She has two children and brought over clothes she wore when she was pregnant, and we re-made them to fit me. I weigh 128 pounds now. Mrs. Arcana will come and help me deliver the baby.

Kevin is ready for a baby. I asked him if we could name the baby, if a girl, Rita Ann like Mrs. Arcana. He likes that name; but if it is a boy, he wants his father's name Michael with a second name of Joseph. I like the name very much because Joseph was Jesus's father's name

Karena was going to have a baby once a long time ago, but she miscarried in the fifth month, and felt it was a sign from God. Kevin does not want to anger God, but he wants this baby in his arms. I told him the baby will come when it is ready.

May is hot and I have gained another four pounds. Kevin says he will call Mrs. Arcana when it is time. Karena is such a good friend. I will miss her when and if they move-they are going to inspect a hot climate and will be gone two months.

10 PM The pains are twenty minutes apart. Kevin called Mrs. Arcana and she came. Eighteen hours later Rita Ann was born.

She is just beautiful and perfect. I love her so much. Mrs. Arcana was so happy we named our baby after her. She is very small, but pretty. She has lots of hair and long fingernails.

Chapter 24

Growing

It has been three months since our baby Rita Ann was born, she is such a delight. Kevin goes crazy when she smiles at him. Karena has been teaching me how to make telephone calls and appointments for Kevin. She wrote it all down on paper. I made nineteen calls today and he has seven appointments.

Mrs. Arcana brought over a small bed cradle-she called it a bass-set cradle. It is nice and the baby fits. That is just until we can afford a crib. Kevin laughed-he told her we had been using a drawer until we find something. He pulled out one of the long drawers on his dresser and sat it on a folding table with a towel inside. Boy am I happy we are not using that for the baby anymore!

Chapter 25

Friends

Carol is moving too-she is the lady down the street with the pear tree. Every time they have pears, I get bushels. Carol taught me to can. I sell the pears too-it helps. We met when I took the baby for a walk. Her daughter wants Carol her to live with them and help watch their children. Sounds nice. She will still be able to visit every now and then.

She brought over stuff: a nice wood crib that has its own mattress and sheets and a blanket. I love it. She brought blankets to wrap the baby and little socks and t-shirts and plastic pants and a christening dress. I called Father Joel; he will come on Sunday and have dinner with us and then Baptize Rita.

I made six appointments for Kevin so far this week and he sold insurance to all those people. Either I am getting the hand of this, and he is a great salesman. He says we are a teamwork.

Chapter 26

Time and Growth

It has been two and a half years since I wrote in this book. I am due in September. Mrs. Arcana had to move near her youngest daughter; but her sister Vi is genuinely nice. She visits me every week and brings bread-this week it was zucchini bread. Rita loves her and likes all her breads. She gives me the recipes. I have quite a book of recipes.

Vi is teaching us how play cards. I play rummy with Kevin and Rita, and it is fun. This is a different kind of pregnancy from when I had Rita. I think I have a boy-but I will not tell that to anyone-just in case it is not a boy. I don't want to get Kevin's hope us-he adores Rita, but a boy would finish our family nicely.

Chapter 27

We are Growing

September 12

This is getting difficult. My leg is swelling, and I feel like my stomach will burst. This baby wants out and I cannot wait. Karena says we will need to go to the hospital for this one, but I know Vi will come and help me. The baby is due in five days. Karena and Mark are having issues I think she wants a baby.

September 16

No baby today. Kevin was so funny he forgot to put on a belt when he went to work. Yesterday he forgot his socks and left the house in his slippers. We set the bass cradle in our room, and we have a blanket and things Rita used all ready.

September 18 no baby yet

September 20 no baby yet

September 22 no baby yet—

Kevin said, it must be I did not figure dates right but that does not agree with what Vi said.

September 24 no baby yet.

Kevin is so funny every ten minutes he was asking "pain yet?"

September 25 no baby yet.

"I hope it knows how to get out!" Kevin said

September 26 no baby yet but labor started at4AM. Our baby boy was born at 11:45PM in the evening. Vi came about 6:30AM but the baby was not in a hurry. The baby is so handsome. Kevin was going nuts waiting so Vi told him to come in and help—that was perfect. He sat at my head and helped me push. He cried as the hours went by, but he stayed me and when our son was born, he screamed for joy. I was too tired to scream.

Michael Joseph is simply perfect. Kevin grabbed to baby and began cleaning him just like Vi showed him. I never heard Kevin sing before, but he was singing.

Chapter 28

Time Marches On

Our children are the most precious thing in the world; I love them so much. Kevin admits he adores our kids. Three neighbors brought over food and presents when Michael came. We live in such a nice area with great neighbors and friends.

I love every minute of being a mom. I am feeling strange, in two more weeks both my close friends will move far away. I know that God will help me find others. These last eighteen months I am busy all the time with no time to write. Michael is growing he will be taller than Kevin. Rita just loves her brother. They are so close. She goes over and kisses him all day long.

Kevin finished the room in the attic. When the kids grow up a little more Michael will move upstairs. I try to make the best use of my time. Kevin just loves being a father and tutoring the children about God, family, and love.

OMG

It has been five years since I have had time to write. We are doing so good, the house is paid in full, and we have the papers. We take the kids to the Swiss Chalet every so often and they love going out for supper.

Kevin and I talked about the idea of another baby. We decided our family if done. God has really been so good to us. Karena and Mark have a baby boy now-but they are not happy. I can't understand that – Mark has a good business, the baby and Karena are healthy, and they have money. What else do they need to be happy?

No time

I have not had any time to write. I have been taking in sewing I work well with the sewing machine. I now know how to take in a dress, do a hem, and sew buttons.

Carol gave me her old Typewriter and sewing machine. I learned how to type quick with a book from the library.

Chapter 29

Busier than Ever

I now type for Doc Evans. Carol had this typewriter for two years and could not do a thing on it. I am up to 75 words a minute. The doctor pays me $8.00 a week to type his notes and set up his file. When the children are in school I do it all.

This has been a terrible year-people are out of work and in bread lines. Mark says the business is almost non-existent. Kevin got another job washing floors at the local grocery. He does that at night and on Saturdays. He gets $5.00 per week. I am selling all my jars of fruit for $.65 cents each. I have 300 jars currently. I tell people to bring their dishes and they could buy the fruit from the jar. I sold 45 jars of fruit just this week. I still want more jars-we are going to the Goodwill on Saturday.

Things are getting better. Kevin is selling insurance again. Our children are wonderful. They are both doing great in school. Sometimes I read their books this way I feel like I am learning just like they are. I feel tired again. I hope I am not pregnant. Kevin says we could not afford any more children. I do not think I am pregnant-but something is not right.

Chapter 30

It Happens to Mary Jo

I have this little ball on my right breast-I wonder what that is? I will just watch it for now. Karena made an appointment with her doctor-she just did not believe that I still do not have a regular doctor. Our children are healthy, and I do not need a doctor.

So, I saw a doctor he said it was something associated with nursing. He told me to just watch it and come back in a year. It does not hurt so I think I am ok-just tired from doing so many different things. I will be ok.

Chapter 31

What will Happen

Eight months later

I told Carol what the doctor said. She did not think that doctor was right. I do not understand she goes to him. She decided I needed to go to the clinic at the Emergency Hospital. She made an appointment. That is the hospital where the nuns where big white hats.

October

I have little time to do anything these days. Both our children are doing well in school; and I love working with Kevin.

Well, Carol came to day to say good bye today. Her daughter sold the house, and they are all moving to North Carolina. We are never going to visit them, and they say they will not be back to Clayton.

Next week Karena will return from visiting her mother.

Karena has her doctor that I went to before and that is who she wants me to see. I will wait for her to go with me.

I am having a problem with one of the boys on the street. He knocked on the door a year ago and asked for help, he said he was hungry. I gave him some milk, a sandwich and some cookies. Well, he comes over about once a month-always hungry. I don't want him here when my children are around. This boy has troubles and needs help I cannot give him, but he always thanks me for the milk, sandwich and cookies. This last time I think he took my picture; I told him not to come again.

Chapter 32

Doctor's

Well, Rita Ann is in the eighth grade. I am so proud of her and Michael. They both are on the honor roll. I finally made an appointment with Karena' s doctor. He said tests were needed to get answer. I told him to do only the best tests. He called and asked me to meet him at the office. I said it would have to wait because Rita's school begins soon, I need to get her new clothes. We set an appointment for two weeks from now.

The doctor said I have stage four infiltrating cancer whatever that means. He said there is not much he could do but he would try new things. The doctor told me the cancer needs to come out. He did not tell me how or why at first. I told him to take it out, but I have no idea how we will pay for it?

When I told Kevin, he was upset and said let the doctor do whatever needs to be done. We made love again that night. I do so love when he holds me. I am safe in his arms always.

You will never guess-what the doctor did? He cut off both my breasts. The doctor did not say he was taking **off** my breast-I thought it was **just the lump**.

Kevin said it did not matter so long as they took all the harmful stuff out-but it mattered to me.

But this was not what I had in mind. I have no idea how we will pay for it or all. I hate the way my breast looks-I put a rag in the bra pocket, but it does not look nice or feel good. I do not think I will write for a while. I really have no time. Kevin has not seen my chest-he has not held me or made love in a month.

Chapter 33

Mary Jo

I am losing track of days and time. I was in the hospital again-where will we get the money? I feel weak-and fragile. What is happening to me? I want to be here for my children-but I feel strange.

The months just keep going by, and I get weaker and weaker. This chemo makes me so sick. I vomit. Kevin knows I am going to die-but he does not talk about it. I so want to be with my children-to see all the important things like birthdays and do things for their Christmases.

I am teaching Rita how to do things around the house. She is so young. I hate the thought of not being there for her. I know that I cannot last long the pain is getting stronger. I am very weak. It has been almost two years since they took off my breasts. I wonder if this is what killed my mother. I pray it will not take my Rita.

I love the way my Rita is growing she is so pretty and very capable. She has a good head on her shoulders, and she is so much smarter than I could ever be. Michael just loves his dad and sister. Every day, even at this age, he waits for Kevin to come home from selling insurance.

I taught Rita how to do the laundry today. It will be hard for her when I die-she will have all the household responsibility. The pain is getting stronger, and I am very tired of fighting.

Rest is difficult, I still have so much to teach Rita. Mark, Karena and Adam will be moving south of the city. At least that is their plan, first Mark wants to set up an office there. I do not know why but Mark is giving Kevin this section of the city to sell insurance and he is going to open another office, 100 miles away-time will tell.

I just know we will not see them that often when they move. Too bad they only have Adam they dote so much on Adam the child needs space. Karena is taking him to Pennsylvania for a visit with her sister and her family. I know she and Mark are still having problems. I hoped once they had a baby their issues would be gone but Adam is now nine years old, and they are still having problems. Mark does not seem to appreciate all the help Karena gives. It is a shame because she does so much now.

The biggest problem is that Mark expects much and gives back little. Karena helps with the business, cooks, buys the groceries, shops for whatever they need, takes care of Adam. I do not know what else a wife could do but Mildred, the bookkeeper said Mark was infatuated with his new secretary. That really must hurt Karena, all the years she helped Mark and believed in him. The girl is only 30 years old and married. Mildred says they do not have children and the girl is getting a divorce. That idea of divorce seems cruel for the wife who helped so much giving love and trust so completely given. It is totally against what is right, fair, and just. I wish men did not always look for greener grass.

What a shame. I am so happy with my Kevin. He would never divorce me-he absolutely loves me and his children.

time is not on my side. Kevin says, I am getting better-but he knows-as I do-I will not be getting better. Michael is so young; I am not sure what he can do to help my Rita. So much will be put on my beautiful daughter I feel guilty being ill for so long. It has been over three years since the doctor found the cancer.

I am going to write a letter to each of my children so they will have something of my thought when am gone. I will put them in my journal. I will write another one for each coming holiday while I am here.

December 2nd ---I always forget to date

I called Father Joel at St Ann's to thanked him for agreeing to officiate at my mass and funeral. He is so kind to us, each week my name is in as sick asking for prayers. It is just a matter of time then; I will be with the Lord. I asked him to help my family. They will need love and prayers. I will have my last mass in his church.

A letter to each of my children is done; I told them how much I love them. I asked them to help their father and be good to him. He is young and will need another wife. It will be hard for him if they become a problem. I ask them for my sake, be kind.

I am tired of being sick. I put the letters in the journal where they will for sure see it. I have not told Kevin about the journal, but it is in the seat of my sewing machine in the attic. He may find the book later...

Kevin took us all out to dinner he borrowed a car from Mark. I guess he is going to buy the car. It is ok, we have been going in a cab to the hospital; a car will save money. I feel terrible to put such a burden on Kevin. I love him very much; he is incredibly good to me. Yesterday, he tried to help me take a bath. He got the towels and set them close to the tub, he made sure a mat was on the floor and he filled the tub. So far, he cannot look at my naked body, he has not since I lost breasts nor can I.

December 28th

I made it through Christmas, which was good. Rita and I cooked together. Rita made the ham and Kevin boiled the sweet the potatoes. Michael set the table it was a quiet day and nice. I gave Mrs. Quackenbush money to do my holiday shopping. She found a nice tie for Kevin, Michael got a tool kit; he loves to fix things, and she found the book he wanted to read. Rita was my most difficult. It was time she had a better bra. She went to Grants with Mrs. Quackenbush and they fitted her. She has two bras now. She is a young lady, and she needed girl things. We talked about certain things, a while ago, she understood everything I told her. She is so beautiful. I regret I will not be around to see her marry and have children of her own. She is good in school. I told her to finish high school before she even thinks of boys. This way when she goes for a job, she will have that diploma. I wish I had one a diploma. I never found the time to take the test.

March 7th

My days are numbered; I have so much I want to write but even that is difficult because I am too ill.

Rita does everything; cooking every day and cleaning. I feel she could manage things. She even does all the grocery shopping.

March 29th

The time is getting closer for me to be with God. Today I began bleeding from my bowl and food does not taste good let alone stay down. Water is the only thing I can drink. I asked Kevin not to let the children's last picture of me be in a burial box. He agreed. I told him time is short and it will happen; I told him to find another wife it is okay with me. He argued but understood.

April 2nd

Life is leaving me. Oh, how I love my family, but God has been good giving me time to teach Rita. Sleep is what I crave now. I cannot write another page.

I spoke to Kevin; I asked him to be sure both our children finish high school-that is important. He promised and while we were talking, he cried. He knows I do not have much time left. I hate leaving him—help him Lord to find another wife a good woman.

God gave us four years to get ready, and now the day is here. Lord thank you for letting me have time to train my daughter. Please take care of my family. I am going to the hospital and will see you soon.

Your loving child,
Mary Jo Wilson

Mary Jo died April 2ⁿᵈ.

That was the last entry; Mary Jo died at 8PM in the Clayton Hospital. Kevin was alone with her when she passed away.

He came home at 10 PM and told the children. Kevin arranged her funeral with a closed coffin. One hundred people were at her service.

Hello, I am Betty Wilson Kevin's second wife; I will try to write things that happened since her death; for Kevin's grandchildren.

Chapter 34

Back to Today

Ava felt the journal gave her a chance to know her great grandmother and how much she loved her family and suffered with cancer. Ava was amazed at their struggles and strange she could not tell anyone her secret. Ava said aloud "I hoped you saw your mother in heaven great grandma."

Ava put the journal away and decided to wait before reading until later. She was reading for five hours and needed to get ready to meet her mother for dinner.

Kurt was out of town on business and would not be back for two days. She was meeting Greta at the Star Point dining room on Main St. She loved eating and shopping together with her mother. Star Point's food is always delicious; the rice pudding is the best in the world and of course there dining room is were in the most elegant restaurant in the world.

After dinner, the ladies planned to shop at the new "mall" that opened with fancy named stores. Shopping is the best remedy for boredom. Ava never mentioned finding the journals to Greta. She wanted to read them first-like her own insight into the family she never knew.

The ladies ate and shopped; Greta suggested they make a day of it and go to theater. It was a long movie "Gone with the Wind," and the ladies were tired at the end. Greta hailed a cab and dropped Ava off at her house and then went ahead home.

Chapter 35

Thanksgiving

Days went by quickly for Ava; the holidays would be upon them and. Ava was talking to Kurt about a day when they could invite everyone over for a party. Greta called Ava and said she would not be in Clayton for Thanksgiving.

She did not mention that Kurt planned a surprise for Ava. Greta was in on it. She told Ava she was going to New York to see friends.

The truth was Ava always wanted to be in New York for the Thanksgiving Day Parade. Kurt arranged for the three of them to meet in New York as a surprise for Ava. All Kurt needed to do was get Ava there.

Ava said, "Mom and I have always been together for the holidays" Greta told Ava, "You too have a new life now and I feel like I am interfering with your lives. I am only going to be gone two days." Ava felt deflated. Kurt said, "Ok honey this is our time and the two of us are going to see the Macy Day Parade in New York. Kurt really did not want to go anywhere least of all New York City on a holiday; but after he planned the surprise, he could not back down, anyway Greta was already in New York. Ava agreed and it was settled.

They were staying at a hotel near Time Square. Their plane arrived at Kennedy Airport about 3 PM. Kurt had supper all planned at a famous restaurant. They arrived at 7 PM for dinner. They were at the table about three minutes when Kurt said, "I have a surprise for you Ava look who is here."

Just then Greta walked to the table. "Oh Mom! Mom!" the two women hugged as Greta told Ava that

Kurt planned the whole thing. New York was just beautiful the shops were all decorated for the holidays and the Macy's Parade was fantastic, as always. The parade hit the top this year for creativeness and beauty. They went to a couple of plays-ate at great restaurants and really enjoyed their time in New York or so it seemed.

This November was very cold in Clayton it snowed two days straight. On their last day in New York Kurt said he needed to discuss something serious with Ava and he wanted to do it as soon as they were home and settled. Kurt did little with his family, in fact during last winter his uncle and his new wife moved to Arizona.

He felt that Ava's relationship with her mother was too close, he wanted to set things in motion immediately. He was against spending all holiday time together with Greta.

Chapter 36

Christmas

Back in Clayton

Kurt said. "Ava, I want to discuss something; I would like to go to Arizona and visit my uncle and his new wife-just the two of us for Christmas. You liked my thanksgiving surprise please do this one for me. I cannot stand to have to spend every holiday with Greta anymore.

Ava was visibly upset, "Kurt, my only real family is my mother, I could not abandon her or leave her out for a holiday let alone for Christmas. We could do what we always do and be with mom over Christmas and then visit your uncle for a couple of days after Christmas. Why suddenly, this issue?

Kurt was in no mood to discuss. He thought that his surprise for Thanksgiving would make this trip happen. He responded,

"Since you feel that way, I will get work completed over Christmas. I will not be having dinner with you and her mother."

Have a good holiday.

This was the first real argument the couple had since they met. All their years together Kurt never mentioned not liking to be with Greta for a holiday or anytime. In past holidays, they always split their time having dinner with Greta then traveling to see Kurt's uncle and his wife.

Now, married less than six months this was the first time Ava heard Kurt talk about not wanting to spend a holiday with Greta. His feelings were too negative, and Ava was puzzled.

Greta knew something was wrong when she called Ava; The tone of her daughter's voice when she answered put her on notice: "Are you ok Ava? What is wrong" Ava was protecting Kurt when she said, "I am just upset Kurt just told me he needs to work on Christmas."

It was fortunate American Airlines agreed to refund Ava's half of the tickets Kurt bought to Arizona. Kurt's new plan was to fly to Arizona without telling Ava on Christmas day. He wanted her to feel his pain for not listening to what he wanted to do. His ticket had a return in four days.

Chapter 37

Trouble

Kurt left the house early on Christmas morning without leaving a note. He did not call Ava on Christmas Day. She dialed him four times at the office with no answer. Finally, when Kurt arrived in Arizona it was late in the day in Arizona, and he called Ava. Their conversation was short-he said "I am in Arizona for visiting my uncle. I told you I wanted to be here for Christmas, you chose to be with your mother. I will be back in four days."

Nothing in that conversation sounded like a newly married man let alone a man in love. Conversation over-Kurt just hung up-not even a goodbye.

Ava called Greta in tears telling her the whole story. Greta told Ava to pack a bag they would be gone for four days to New York. They arrived at 6 PM Christmas Day.

They went to a late dinner with a person Greta wanted Ava to meet. Ava presumed she would be meeting Dr. Cantor as that was the name on the registered letter Greta received and was Greta's friend.

Greta did not tell Ava anything except that she was meeting an old friend. Seated at the restaurant a tall man came to the table it was Mr. Cantor. Ava leaned over and said to Greta "He is very attractive, mom." Dinner conversation was about Slade West. Mr. Cantor said, "Ava, I am happy to finally to meet you. I was not only a longtime friend of your father's, but I was also his attorney. We met when I moved my family next door to him and his family. Your father had a little girl and a wife-both passed away too young. You dad was a paramedic for many years."

Ava asked "Do you know how my father died? I would love an opportunity to hear everything about my dad." Mr. Cantor mentioned "I am planning on going to Clayton soon I would love to have dinner just the three of us. But now I have an appointment and need to leave. Greta, I will call you when my plans for going to Clayton are firmed up, Goodbye Ava it was nice to meet you." Ava said "Goodbye, I look forward to our next dinner in Clayton when I could learn about my father."
Mr. Cantor left.

Back in Clayton Ava presumed this was a "relationship between Mr. Cantor and Greta." She was shocked when Greta said he was only a friend. Mr. Cantor flew into Clayton two weeks later and Greta invited Ava to join them at dinner. Greta told Mr. Cantor previously said she "was concerned about Ava and Kurt; something is not right with them." She felt "it is time to tell Ava that she could take care of herself." Mr. Cantor said he understood.

Chapter 38

It's Time

Mr. Cantor was a handsomely dressed man with a suede blue jacket, a white turtleneck sweater, and dark blue pants. His silver hair was a great touch. After dinner and pleasantries, Ava asked Mr. Cantor how he and her mother met. Mr. Cantor replied "Ava, I mentioned I was your father's friend and his attorney. When he died, I read his will to your mother. She was pregnant with you at that time." Ava asked, "How did my father die? Was he terribly ill? How long did you know my father? Greta interrupted, "Ava, Mr. Cantor wants to tell you something about your father's will and what he left for you."

Mr. Cantor explained her father's will the first he left you was the medical center. It was put in trust with a caretaker. The caretaker had an option to purchase the building; Greta as executor and your trustee, recently sold the building to the caretakers. The sale provides you a mortgage on the property for fifteen years at a nice interest rate." He then proceeded to explain "Greta will be turning over parts of the trust to you every five and ten years according to your father's plan which permitted Greta to have use of the funds as long as she is alive."

It was an unbelievable shock to Ava. She responded to Mr. Cantor explaining her father's will, "Do you mean to tell me, that all the time my mom had me working through high school and college, watching every penny I spent—all of it could have been paid for? Do you mean we lived on a small allowance on PURPOSE when I could have had anything I WANTED? Do you mean my father left me a fortune and...

Greta was shocked and decided to put a stop to it: "Ava, I gave you values, a normal life not flaunting money in your face. I helped you understand the value of family, education, and an appreciation for what you had been given and you did take care of everything you had. I provided you an exposure to the world with travel not to mention the ability you now have with a college degree and be able to care for yourself and to be a productive member of society. I gave you 100% of my attention thanks to your father's money. I protected your future with selling Mr. Cantor's daughter Dr. Cantor the building she and her mother took car of for twenty-one years. Her mortgage will provide you with a bonus for fifteen years to come. I cannot believe your comments, instead of being thankful for everything you have the nerve."

Ava interrupted: "Did you think that letting me go through high school and college years working and trying so hard to stretch my funds were funny mother? Did you laugh at my stress? Your behavior was cruel, selfish, and controlling to have done that to me—just the stress alone was cruel."

Greta said, "I have really given you everything you needed and wanted-yes I made you consciously aware of money and if this is how you are reacting, I am glad you never knew what your father left for you."

This was the first time Ava treated her mother with such distain. Greta did not know her daughter at that moment. Mr. Cantor tried to help Greta, but he was to be New York that evening and needed to catch a plane; he left to grab a cab to the airport. He told Greta he would call her.

On the ride home from dinner the ladies barely spoke. It was three days before Ava called her mother and their conversation was brief. Ava said she was just "checking in." she mentioned nothing about having told Kurt of her financial situation.

Meanwhile Kurt was furious "We spent five months renovating this old house when we could have built a new house. Well now neither one of us need to dread going to work every day. Do you know what this means, you have money. I cannot believe your stingy cruel mother. All she wanted was control-control over you and your money. You need to take control over your own money, and ready to control your own trust."

Ava was totally and completely confused at Kurt's reaction. But even more shocked when the next day he quit his job. He told her he wanted to have his own business. Her whole life had changed, and she was not sure how or why things were happening. Kurt was like a stranger to her now. They did not hug, kiss or make love. Kurt came in for dinner and left in the morning. He told her he was looking for a building. This went on for two weeks until one day Ava was so distraught went to Greta's house and asked if they could talk.

Greta had no idea what her daughter was going through-in fact, she would have never guessed that Kurt would behave in the manner he was showing.

Ava spoke openly to her mother about her situation with Kurt. Greta was not sure what to do. Ava wanted to do whatever Kurt wanted-and if was a building then she wanted him to have it and she wanted Greta to give her the money.

In two months, according to Slade's will, Ava will have the benefit of the mortgage money from the medical building. It was no small sum, but it was money coming in monthly. Kurt must have thought the whole amount was available and belonging to Ava at this time rather than a fifteen-year mortgage.

Greta estimated that the first move would be in five years unless there was a major health issue. In this was the way it would remain in effect to take care of Greta. The estate has always been growing. The original estate has more than tripled thanks to Greta's business sense and ability. The estate unequivocally left Greta in control.

Chapter 39

Life Changes

Ava was distraught Kurt wanted money to develop his own business; he wanted Ava to control her money. Greta wanted to give Kurt a mortgage on any property he wanted to buy with monthly payments being made to her. He said, "NO mortgage."

Ava said "I love him, and I cannot stand the fighting. What is the money for if not to have happiness?"

This was Greta's only child and if money would make her life happier, she decided she would transfer some funds to Ava once Kurt found a building. The next morning Kurt called about noon: he found a building for 1.2 million dollars. He wanted to buy it and he wanted

Ava to get the money from her mother. Fearful she was losing her marriage and the love of her life she called Greta and asked for the funds.

Greta said it would take a week, but she would give her the money for the building Kurt wanted. Kurt persisted "Your mother will still be controlling you-and your money." This was a side of Kurt Ava did not understand. She warned Ava that giving him this money would be the beginning of money being more important to him than her.

Ava did not care-or believe that would happen all she wanted was her husband back. She was feeling lost and wanted to do whatever to make Kurt happy. He wanted to own the building and not have any pressure to grow his paper business. He promised Ava this it would give them a normal business. Kurt wanted to buy and sell paper products.

After a couple of days, the transfer of cash was made to Ava's account. Kurt bought the building and re-negotiated the sale price. He told Ava he needed start-up money. The building was in his name alone and the rene-gotiated price was $800,000.

After the sale Kurt came home with flowers and a pearl necklace for Ava. Meanwhile Kurt said she should leave her job. He wanted her home and with no financial strain so it might be time to begin a family. Ava was overjoyed. Just the idea of a baby changed Ava. It took three months for Ava to get pregnant. She and Kurt were overjoyed. Ava began feeling as if they would finally return to the love they enjoyed before she told Kurt about the estate. Unfortunately, Ava miscarried in her third month. She was devastated. Her doctor assured her there would be another chance for a baby. Miscarriage was a normal way for the body to say something was wrong. It was a tough time for Ava, and she retreated to reading the journals she placed in her basement.

Kurt was busy and after her miscarriage. Ava was feeling lonely. Rita was not feeling well, Greta went to Chicago. She would only be gone a week. Ava decided to read the next journal from the box. The next journal began in a very strange way:

The Journals were numbered, and she read the first and then the eighth now she was reading #2

Hi, my name is Betty Hewitt. As a young girl I kept a diary and when I got to be 21 years old, I destroyed it –for privacy reasons. I lived with my mother for all 36 years of my life. My father left us when I was just a baby. My mother did not have any faith in men after that, she did not like me even dating. All I ever did was work. I met a man at work, a widower. I knew little about his wife, but I knew he had a terrific daughter who could pass as my child. I marred Kevin Wilson six years after his first wife Mary Jo died and eight months after my mom died.

He seemed like a nice man but strange. He did not really flirt or try to pick me up. He just became a friend stopping occasionally to say "Hi." One day he asked me out for coffee. I told him "I was never out with a man before." He liked that, and we hit it off.

We began going out on nights his daughter was in school. He loved that "I was exclusive-whatever that meant." We fell in love.

Kevin and I told my mother that we were getting married, and she really threw a fit. Kevin and I argued, and we separated. His stubbornness led to a confrontation with his daughter Rita, and she left him and moved in with me.

Kevin ended up getting drunk every weekend for six months after Rita left. Rita needed a specific dress, stopped at the house, and found drunken Kevin on the floor with his hand bleeding. Rita and I both tended to him. It was all over in that shower-we finally got past all that nonsense and realized we were in love and love took over. We married within a week. I love him very much. I think he finally understands why we needed to wait, and he does not hold it against me.

Kevin is a great worker. All the things I wanted to have done in mother's house was now getting done. The house looks terrific. Rita lives in Kevin's old house. While Ava and I were living together, we became great friends. She is not just a friend she is like a daughter. I hope Michael will be a "son" when he returns from the army.

I will be able to write details of our lives. We are busy people. Still, I want to update this journal. Michael and Nora married just as planned.

Almost two years have gone bye. I know I should be writing about all stuff, but I get so involved in different things. Kevin and are traveling and since time just flies when you are having fun—I forgot about writing in the journal.

The following will be a brief review: Lilly, Nora's aunt and guardian wanted new things done to update her house, because Nora was pregnant. The carpenter she hired was a widower. They fell in love and married, and she now lives in his home.

1. Nora and Michael were high school sweethearts. When he came back from the war in Germany, he was a different person. Still, they married and had a baby girl and named her, Greta. She is a doll. Michael picked the name.

2. Michael still acts a bit strange always wanting to control everything. He watches Nora and sits or walks away but never pitches in and helps her. It must be difficult for her.

3. Kevin, and George- (Lilli's husband)-entered a carpentry business. They want Michael to join their business one day. Kevin and George like each other and are like brothers.

    Life has been good for Lilly and George

4. Rita's friend- was shot during a robbery. He was a hero but will never be the same. Rita said he moved out of town to live with his mother.

5. Rita and Nora both graduated college and became a teacher. Nora loves being a mom-and Greta is just precious. Michael loves the baby so much. Rita loves being an aunt. She will be a terrific mother

6. But, something bad happed to Rita A man forced his way into her house and raped her. The man, beat her badly, cut one side of her hair, bit her

breast and ransacked the house. Rita was passing out when the policeman arrived. The policeman picked up Rita and took her to the hospital in the police car. Rita was in the hospital for a week then stayed with Michael and Nora. While in hospital she met a young doctor whose sister was raped. He understood how to oversee things like this and brought her to a councilor.

7. Michael and Kevin made a comment that it happened on a Sunday-and Rita went out for a walk even though all the stores are closed due to the Blue Laws. Rita did not want to return to school this year. When school was to open again the principal asked her to return and gave her a light load that year.

What Rita does not know is that Michael secretly told her principal about the rape. Rita did not want anyone to know she was out alone on a Sunday. I think that stuff is silly but who can argue with their Catholic upbringing.

Another year has passed. My house is work, I asked Kevin for a smaller house. I like Rita's house we will see if she would exchange houses. I am concerned about the man that raped her.

Kevin and George's construction business is growing. It was Kevin and Michael's love for each other that made Michael joined them in business. It is nice feeling to have such a good family. We are all "tight" if you know what I mean. I am the luckiest person in the world to have a family who respects each other and loves being together often.

Well summers is over everything went well this time. Being a newlywed we both need to adjust our life-styles and get used to each other. It is still so new we are both working on these things.

Carl is the name of the doctor Rita met while in the hospital, he has been spending time with her lately encouraging her to see his friend. His friend is a rape councilor. After many discussions she agreed to see his friend. The councilor and Rita were communicating regularly. Then, just after Christmas Carl asked her to marry him. How romantic.

Michael acted strange, one day, Nora was planning to take the baby outside to play in the snow; he felt it was too cold and took the baby from Nora hands. Then he told her not to tell him how to parent. The baby cried-but in the end Michael won and the baby stayed inside. He told Nora "When I make a decision, I do not expect you to disrespect my decision. I said it was too cold for the baby to be out at this time."

Wow we all thought that is a bit tough.

You'll never guess right after Rita and Kevin decided that we could swap houses; Carl aske Rita to marry him. Not only that but Carl and Rita married quickly. Carl wanted changes in our house, but he had no money. Kevin agreed to do three of the minor changes.

I really enjoy having a smaller house to clean. It was also closer to the bus; with Nora and Michael close by it was a good decision.

This has been an extremely busy time:
First there was: the holidays,
Then swapping of houses,
Then Rita and Carl wedding.

I hope everything works out for Rita and Carl. Carl is not Catholic and does not appreciate any of the pomp and circumstance that goes on in a church.

No one from Carl's his family attended the wedding.
He never mentions his family. Everything he has goes to pay his schooling.

Kevin has made changes in Rita's house for me. I am so happy he takes my suggestions. I love him so much. We put my house in Rita's name alone-Kevin thought it would be better that way. I am so happy we swapped houses.

September 10th

Yesterday I was moving things into the attic. Kevin always says he will take things to the attic, but he was working late. There are some strange hinges on an area and no doorknob. I called Rita and she said there was a room that Kevin built after Mary Jo's death. He only showed her when Nora was having Greta.

If Rita has a child, I hope it's a girl. I love being called a "Grandmother" Kevin said "Consider the room as your sewing retreat! But hopefully only when I am not home, I because when I am home, I want you all to myself."

Kevin and George are making their business legal. They are naming it "K & G Construction." If Michael ever joins, they will and "& Son" that is so nice.

I had a great holiday. Kevin is so romantic at times-I feel like I am a queen.

I am so happy loving Kevin. Thank you, God.

Chapter 40

Lil

Greta is growing like a weed. No one could say anything to Michael when he is disciplining the child or Nora, he gets terribly upset. Nora cannot even discuss his parenting, or he jumps down her throat. I tried to suggest something, and Michael blew up. I asked Kevin if we could leave, and we did-but Kevin does not want me to suggest anything to Michael.

Nora called yesterday and apologized for Michael. Everything to him is about respect. There are times Nora walks on eggshells. She said, "Living this way has been harder since Greta was born."

My lunch with Lil was difficult, she is worried about George's heart. The doctor said his heart is not strong. Lil is determined to take him to Arizona and get him to rest. We will see.

Lilly is such a doll she is like a kid in love for the first time. She said she has a secret about something that worries and torments her. She prays God will forgive her every day. In my heart I feel, Lil is too gentle a lady to ever have done anything bad

June 8th

Greta is precious. I really miss not having children. Her birthday party was super. She so loves everyone.

Rita had a baby girl; her name is Shana. It was Carl's grandmother's name, and he loves the name. Lilly gets to watch Greta and I will get to watch Shana

Nora must check everything with Michael. She loves him very much but that makes for such a strain in a marriage. Talking things out is always a gift. Michael is thinking of joining Kevin and George, I wonder how that will work.

George is a genius with kids he hired a group to shovel driveways and they call themselves the "G men." It is a joy to see George and Lilly together they are truly soul mates.

Kevin thinks he is fat. I must cut down on oil, butter, trim our meat more and add more vegetables to our food and watch making pies. We have been so tired lately we seem to have lost doing fun things we once enjoyed." Nora mentions I should not always do what Kevin wants. I just want peace and love. Michael gets angry with me. He is short tempered just like Kevin has been.

Yes, it has been a long time. The doctor said I have high blood pressure. I wonder if one could get high blood pressure from being lonely. The doctor says stress causes many things.

Kevin can do anything he puts his mind to do. Our relationship is changing. What happened to all the attention and fun we used to have- I wonder if this happens to other wives.

There are times we agree in private but later he does the opposite.

Well school is out, and Shana will be with Rita again for the summer. I love having her and will miss her." Rita has her call me every night and say: "good-ite" it is so cute. I thank Rita for that kindness. Rita and Carl have a different relationship lately. When I asked her about it, she just said Carl is working so many hours.

Two months later September 1

When Michael wants every new piece of equipment he just goes out and buys this makes George and Kevin get aggravated. He spends company money and then finds out that the equipment is not what he thought and then he wants to give it away—what is he thinking?

Chapter 41

A New Year

September 3

Shana is so mature for her age. She just loves Greta, and they get along like sisters. I make clothes for the girls, occasionally, and they love to dress like sisters.

November 2nd

Time passes so quickly. Thanksgiving was not a good day. I was very frightened; a man who I suspect was the man the raped Rita, was waiting for someone near our house. Kevin tried to follow him in the car but lost him-I a very frightened and do not want to stay in this house anymore. We called the police. We are going to Michael's.

Something happened about a month ago that also makes me want to move. I was coming into the bedroom about 10PM; I opened the door Kevin was half asleep. but he called me Mary Jo. Add that to the issue of the rapist and this will be my last entry written in this house.

We all came back to the house for Thanksgiving Day, but it became day of terror. Something no one would ever have suspected could happen or was possible. A strange man came into the yard where the children were playing, he called to Judy and after she came to him, he put a knife into her chest. Judy is nine years old. Thank God, Carl was here, when the police car arrived, Carl had Judy in his arms and he got in and told the policeman to "take us to the hospital, I am a doctor." Another police-man came to the house and spoke to the children. They are all young and frightened.

I asked Kevin to sell the house. Kevin said "OK." Michael will find a real estate man. We now need to find another house. I would like to be near a bus line; and I really would like to have a fireplace and place for my sewing machine and these books.

December 17th

Well, we have a new house. We got a real deal because the house was vacant. The Real estate man spoke to the attorney for the sellers -they live in a different state now- and the attorney gave us permission to for us to do the work in the new house before we close. He is just terrific!

May 19th

Easter brought good news-the man that raped Rita is dead. His name was Dell something or other and he was the son of a man that was married to one of their neighbors. He had mental problems and was a bad person; he was the one that stabbed Judy. Now we do not have to worry any longer. It was a relief for all of us.

July 10

My life has been changing. Kevin and Charlie have a strained relationship. He gets along great with John, but Charlie always does his own thing?

Kevin tells me that I have opinions on everything. Without an opinion one lacks values and without structure and values one becomes passive. If that happens your life and the lives of those you are with-becomes a facade and you end up always blaming someone else for the results.

The Bible says: "And the two shall become one" that becoming is the real problem. I thought we should be a team not just one.

December 7th,

I know time is going by and I have not been writing –but you see so much of our lives have changed. Michael is not firmly planted working with George and Charlie.

The time is going by so quickly. Carl, Rita and Shana now will live in Chicago. They will be leaving in a week. It was all done so fast. They even bought a house in Chicago.

Carl has a new hospital in which to develop his burn cream.

February 12th

Letter today from Rita. It was a shocker. She is questioning what she did not see about Carl. in the past?

I am happy, Kevin never showed me a jealous streak or one looking for the ultimate in control. It seems so many people argue. Isn't marriage supposed to be a safe zone where you give, take, and learn to become one in the eyes of God? Aren't people supposed to learn from each other without resentment and hatred? What happens to people- it seems mostly men? They love watching young girls on the TV-it gets their juices flowing, and they fail to appreciate their wives.

Lately young girls are showing too much body. Boobs are now being shown on TV and about every movie star today sees nothing wrong with showing their breasts, full legs and more. What does that teach young girls? Is anyone ever going to be a role model for decency. Kevin an old fart-says "Women just need to go with the flow. It would be best if they tried to keep looking like the women on TV then men would appreciate them better. Try doing just that!"

I think that statement was stupid. Hollywood stars are not the housewife reality, cooking, cleaning, shopping, taking care of the house, the family, and many work outside the home—but who could tell Kevin anything.

John developed a security program. Everyone wants one, this could be the beginning of something big for the company.

June 9th.

So many things have happened this is just a quick rundown. The business started with George; John really made that security stuff into a great business, Charlie's crew monitors signals and notifies the police of an attempt to break in happens. That part of the business is also growing like a weed. George thinks that the business should be divided three ways when he dies. George and Kevin's share will go to Michael. The other two share one John and the other to Charlie.

Michael does not want any more children. Rita was pregnant again, but she also miscarried.

August 15,

Can you imagine how great it is to feel loved?
I can. I just think everyone in the world should know the feeling. Last night was a rare occurrence. Kevin wanted to make love-and it was terrific. He was enthusiastic, tender, and loving; it was something I missed for so long. I hope he stays this way. It is what makes everything right-when you feel important to someone, and love is in the picture. Please God don't let this change again!

November 20th

Michael and Nora are having words again over Greta. Carl is fixed only on Shana, Rita is no longer important—I am exaggerating a bit. Time will tell.

December 30th

Well, everyone was in for the holidays.

Nothing changes these days-and there is little to write. I am to check Charlie's house when he leaves for his son's funeral. They brothers keep the house clean, and everything looked good. Kevin hates that I help the boys out when I can. But it gives me something to do and nice people to talk with, and they appreciate my help.

I am working at the church. There is a nice man there he complements me all the time. He is a friend of the church's housekeeper. Those few compliments make me feel nice, he says "I look pretty" or "You always have something special to say" or "My, you really are quite efficient." Sometimes he calls me "Sunshine" and I like that. It is a lonely world and when a stranger can make you feel like a person and your husband who you love does not complement you.

I introduced John to Maggie she is a widow. She has no children and lives alone. I think it is a perfect match! When John came to church, he and Maggie hit is off-just as I predicted! He asked her out for coffee, and they left together. Wow I might be a match maker.

Michael decided he wants them to be staying home on certain nights pending on what is on the television. The television is now taking over family time -why?

Feb. 8th

I went to New York with three of the girls from the church. We drove there and were gone five days. We all did the driving. I like New York there was always something to do. Marjorie-is the oldest– she is fifty-seven years old. She has been to New York every year for the last thirty years. She knew all the best spots to see a show or buy clothes and even where the best place there is to eat. We had a wonderful time. I am ready to take this trip anytime they want to go.

We arrived home Sunday at 9 PM. It was a long drive, but we all talked and had fun. Kevin was waiting up for me. I think he missed me because he gave me a hug and kiss and in bed, he showed me that I was still attractive to him. When he holds me, I feel alive and when he makes love to me, I feel so much a part of him. I hope this continues. He is the man of my dreams. I seem to dream about him all the time.

Something strange has been happening I am not feeling so well. I will call the doctor.

November 16th

Went in to see the doctor and well, this is a shocker, I need to watch sugar and carbs. I am 22-pounds overweight, and I am on a diet. Until I get the weight down, I need to be careful.

January 29th.

Well, you guessed it-I ate Christmas cookies and gained six pounds. I am back on the diet and this time I will not cheat.

I received the strangest letter from Rita. She wrote

"Life is strange. I am not alone. I am getting rid of frustration and finding the Lord."

Not sure what that all means.

Rita has been acting sort of different-I mean she is keeping more to "herself." Her letters and calls are getting rare I wonder if they are having problems. Shana is so beautiful I know they want another baby but ---who knows what goes on in the minds of people these days.

The last two weeks I have not been able to figure Kevin out-I thought cooking, cleaning, grocery shopping, laundry, being there-helping-sharing and caring-giving him all my thoughts and energy was enough-believe me I fail at every step. Kevin wants the house to look like a picture-but I want it to be comfortable and used. If we had lots of company that would be what I wanted but family is our main entertainment, and they want comfort and a lived-in environment.

Chapter 42

Strange and Funny

Ava put the journals away she completely forgot the time. She was reading for almost five hours. Kurt was late he was due home an hour ago. She jumped out of her chair and ran into the kitchen to cook something. She found rice, a nice piece of chicken, asparagus and then decided to make a stir fry dish. It was almost 8 PM when Kurt called "I am sorry, I forgot the time. I hope you had supper?" Ava had fallen asleep on the sofa and did not eat. She asked Kurt why he was so late. "Just a business meeting I should be home in an hour-eat something."

It was the third time in a week that Kurt was late. It made Ava curious. She decided to check it out-and just inquire about asking Cara, Kurt's secretary. Cara was 45 years old and a mother of two beautiful daughters Micky 12 years old (Michelle being her real name) and Joy 15 years old. Both girls were truly kind, and respectful to their mother they helped clean the house, cooked and did chores. Cara's husband worked at the steel plant but during the last year he has been terribly ill with a lung infection. Milton was bed ridden much of the time.

Ava and Cara are friends, so this would just be a normal conversation. Ava waited until 4PM and dialed Cara at the office. Cara seemed distant and preoccupied.

She said she would call Ava later. Three hours later Cara returned her call. "Please excuse my abrupt behavior but there were a number of people around my desk" Ava understood. She asked Cara about Kurt's nighttime appointments and about the business. "Ava, I-I am afraid you will need to discuss this with Kurt."

Ava recognized she should have led into her questions differently. So, she changed the topic and went ahead to discuss Cara's girls. Then about fifteen minutes later she asked again, and Cara said "she had not arranged any evening business meetings.

Kurt did not get in until almost 11 o'clock for three nights. He was tired and wanted to just get to bed. Ava was upset and decided this situation needed to be addressed. She had a friend Phillip. Phil was a private detective she had met in college. Phillip was nice and agreed to check the situation and keep her informed. After a week he got back to her. "Ava, this is Phil I want to assure you I found no evidence that Kurt was having an affair." "Well Phil where is he going at night?" she asked. "Ava, he is in school" "What! Why would he not tell me Phil? What is he taking?" "That is the strange part Ava" "What do you mean" "He is taking courses in acting" "What!" "Yes, you heard me-acting. He is in a theater group-they are supposed to have a play coming up in two weeks at the school." "Thank you, Phil."

As their call ended Ava was more perplexed. She wondered why he would not tell her about being in a play. She wondered if he planned to invite her to see the play. Kurt came in late, she asked him "What kind of business are you doing at night so often?" "Well, this is difficult to discuss," he said "but it is about time I tell you. I am taking classes in acting. I am in a play next week."

Surprised at his frankness; Ava decided to pursue. Why didn't you tell me? Am I invited to the play?"

He looked at her and then said "I thought you would think me silly and foolish. I would love for you to come to the play-but still I do not want your mother to find out just—ok?" Kurt was worried of being laughed at or if the acting would be difficult for Greta to accept. The two of them talked for about an hour Ava assured him that she would not let Greta know. That night Kurt made love to Ava thanking her for being so understanding.

The play was not at all what Ava expected. It was a comedy and Kurt was the star comedian. It was funny in a strange sort of way. Kurt has always been a serious individual-why this kind of theater she wondered. On the way home from the play Ava asked Kurt why he chose this class. His answer was shocking, very logical and totally honest. "I am tired of always being told how serious I am or that I am a "stuffed shirt," There were times a client would say "lighten up Kurt" that was terribly frustrating. "So, I decided to learn to use humor as a way of breaking the ice with businesspeople." Shocked Ava said

"I am proud of you Kurt and if tonight was an example of your lightening up-you did simply fine. The show was a success, and you are a natural, I was genuinely surprised."

"Thank you, Ava. I really appreciate that you came tonight. I am fortunate that you are not upset with me for not telling you what I was doing." That evening the two of them teased each other just like old times. They made love and held each other all night. Their discussion really gave Ava a relief she hated doubting him. Trust was how their relationship was built. She loved Kurt and now he was going to even have a funny side. Loving him and laughing at his jokes would be nice. *'As long as he does not make too many jokes" she thought.*

Next thing was to decide on plans for the holidays; Kurt was in still another play. The holidays were almost non-existent as Ava did little shopping or decorating. Kurt was busy studying and rehearsing for another play. Greta accepted another assignment in January and would be gone for a month.

It was April before the light shined in Ava's eyes again after her miscarriage. Ava's thoughts went into high gear. "What is wrong with me. I need to get myself back to me. I really need to snap out of this." On her way home she stopped at Kurt's office he was on the telephone. When he saw the smile on her face, he cut his call and asked Ava about her day. The two talked for a while and then went to lunch. "Kurt, I feel so stupid-thinking my situation was a problem I love you Kurt will all my heart." Ava looked at Kurt and hoped he return the declaration but all he did was put his hand over her hand and say, "I am happy you are better." Kurt's not returning an "I love you" was unsettling for Ava. She made a fried chicken for dinner stuffed dressing and an apple pie. The evening was pleasant but not what she had hoped it would be. Kurt was tired he needed to study his lines for the opening the next day and he was not in the mood for romance.

Chapter 43

New York

Two days later Kurt received a call from the director of the plays at the school. A recruiter seen the last play and wanted to speak with Kurt. He initially asked for his "agent." The director asked Kurt if their recruiter could meet with him over dinner that evening. Kurt agreed and called Ava with the news. Ava was not impressed "This is a course you are taking not a career move-right" she said. Kurt assured her he was doing this just for fun. He promised to tell her all about it when he got home.

Acting was giving Kurt a new focus and she feared he was taking it seriously. It was 11:30 PM when Kurt arrived home. He was all excited. "I was asked to inter-view for the Jerry Lewis Muscular Dystrophy Telethon in

September" he said. "The man Adam Glisten said it was a terrific opportunity and that maybe I could get on one of the late-night shows-isn't that terrific?"

Ava was not excited in fact she was confused and taken back at his enthusiasm and commitment audition for the Telethon. "Where do you have to go to audition?" she asked" "I can do it here in Clayton, there is a station set up right here and if I get to be part of the show I could do it right from that station."

"Aren't you excited?" he asked. "Yes, Kurt that is a nice opportunity and I am happy for you." Ava said tongue in cheek. She wanted him to remember that this was not supposed to be his goal but a way to help him in the business.

That evening Kurt could not sleep he was on the telephone with the director from the school class until after midnight. The next morning, he was out before 8 AM. The next three weeks Kurt was gone much of the time. He was working with the directory on "copy" that was his monologue for the show.

The Jerry Lewis Telethon was on Labor Day. Kurt won four minutes. Ava was in the audience at the station along with the director of the class and everyone in the class. He was good but in Ava's mind not a "Hit." Kurt loved it. One of the acts could not make it so Kurt agreed to go on again in the middle of the night as well. He did not come home until after the telethon was over the next morning.

Kurt was elated the telethon scheduler asked him to volunteer next year as well and he agreed. Ava was sure this would be it. He had his fifteen minutes of fame and now it may be an annual volunteer program. Kurt slept all most all day. It was 8 PM when the director from his class called. He asked him if he would agree to work at a local night club. They could only pay him $50.00 for each 10 minutes of comedy and there would be two for the night. Kurt jumped at the chance and when the conversation was over, he picked up Ava and danced her around the room "I am a star a star!" Ava did not know what to say she was taken back by Kurt's excitement and the offer. Kurt wanted to celebrate "Let's go out" he said but Ava protested; it was 8:30 PM. "I do not care-anyway once I succeed, I will have a lot of night life." Ava did not want to dress up and go out "where do you want to go?" she asked "Out, my love, I have not had dinner and I am hungry."

Ava got dressed it was almost 9:20 PM when they left the house. There was a small club open, and Kurt wanted to stop there. The place was about empty, and the man told Kurt that the kitchen was closed. He said most places would be closed at that time on a Sunday evening. They ended up at a Your Host Restaurant and Kurt had a breakfast special, and Ava just had a piece of pie and tea.

The next three weeks were terribly lonely for Ava. Kurt was working on his monologue, and he was gone most evenings. Then came the night for his performance Ava was there and the place was packed. Kurt was funny, and the audience loved him. All the way home all Kurt could talk about was where would the next gig be. He was sure there were more to come.

No one knew a local reporter at the club the night of Kurt's performance. The reporter surprised everyone and authored an article in the Sunday paper about an "Upcoming Star of Comedy from Our Hometown." Life with Kurt was changing rapidly. Kurt was taking "gigs" at all the local restaurants and clubs.

Ava did not like the night life-she now stayed home. Kurt would come in from performing around 4 AM. There were nights he smelled of alcohol. Within two weeks he was offered five spots and three for a weekly Saturday night "gig." He accepted all the opportunities coming his way for doing shows. His "take" for a ten-minute show went from $50 performance to $150 per performance in less than a month. There were nights if he did three shows, he would make $450. Then a club owner asked him to be exclusive for one week two shows a night and offered him $2000. He took it.

Kurt was not able to go to work on Monday's after performing all week. He was too tired. Then one night after dinner Ava planned to talk about this new direction Kurt was taking when the telephone rang. It was an owner of a club in New York City, and he wanted to hire Kurt for six weeks as an opening act for a singer he had just hired. He offered Kurt all expenses plus $550 for eight minutes each. All he had to do was one show on Friday evenings and two shows on Saturday evenings. He agreed to include a hotel room and a flight. Kurt accepted the job without even talking it over with Ava. "This is my big chance he told Ava-are you coming with me?" Ava had been to New York over twenty times in her life she did not want the night life that was driving Kurt. She asked him if he would fly down on a Friday and return on Sunday. He agreed but after the first two weeks of flying back and forth -he decided to just stay down there until the end of the "gig."

From one gig to the next and it was all Ava could do to keep up appearances. "Yes, he has been having lots of luck lately; Yes, we are very fortunate…." It was all she could do not to scream at every reporter on the telephone that wanted information about Kurt.

Then what Ava feared finally came. It was about midnight when Kurt called. He was at a party and wanted to tell Ava of the great news. "I have signed a contract for thirteen weeks here in New York. I am a success! Why don't you join me?" since it was obvious to Ava this was not the time to discuss this situation, she congratulated him and said they would talk on Friday when he came home.

"Home-Home who is going home. There is no point I took an apartment here. Put the house up for sale and join me?" Ava was stunned. "I do not know what to say Kurt-I have my family I just cannot leave. Why don't you come home for a couple of days, and we will discuss it?"

This was not the Kurt she has been with for almost six years. He never acted like this, and she did not know him, and she hated when he called her "Baby."

"Forget it baby-I am here for thirteen weeks if you want to me-get on a plane. Got to go everyone is waiting to congratulate me-I am at a celebration party. I will call you tomorrow afternoon I will be at the hotel until Monday" and with that he was gone.

This was a difficult situation-at no time in their entire relationship did she ever guess this would be their problem. She dialed Gloria Shorts. Gloria was twenty-six years old blond 5' 4" tall and married to Tom Shorts for the last five years. She was also one of Ava's friends from work. Gloria had known Kurt since he was sixteen years old. She was not at all helpful her whole conversation revolved around the excitement of having a star and living in New York. Her next call was to her cousin Katherine. Katherine had a unique perspective. She asked Ava to consider "What she really wanted in life-was it the magical life of New York or a home and family." Katherine had given up the idea of becoming a country singer when she met her husband. She never regretted getting married or her family. She sings now in the church choir.

After her call Ava wrote down all the reasons, she could think of why the New York star life was not what she wanted. Unfortunately, she loved Kurt and while there had been changes in him since their marriage, she had years with him prior and she felt that this would just be a phase. She decided to go to New York for the weekend and discuss it with him face to face. She arranged a flight for the next morning.

It was 9:45AM when she arrived at the hotel where he was staying. She asked the desk clerk for his room number and a key he told her Kurt's room was 876 but he would have to call to announce her first. She spoke to Kurt on the house phone he asked her to give him about fifteen minutes to clean up the place. A funny feeling came over Ava she decided to go to the 8th floor and see what he was cleaning. As the elevator door opened, she saw Kurt kissing a young lady goodbye and saying he would call her later. The lady had her evening clothes on, and her hair was a mess. Just then Kurt saw Ava and decided to introduce the young woman. "Ava this is Susie-she helps out at the club" it was obvious to Ava that Susie was embarrassed and that Susie may help at the club, but she has other duties.

Kurt said that Susie fell asleep on the sofa, and she was just leaving. That was not what Ava thought and when she went into the apartment noticing that only the bed had been slept in. It was obvious to her that two people had slept in the bed. This was something that Ava did not count on happening.

Kurt had never been a man to flirt let alone even look at another woman since the two of them had met. This wase one of the things being in show business breeds and she wanted no part of it.

When the door to the hotel room was closed, she asked Kurt if he slept with Susie. At first, he denied it but when Ava pointed to the nylons on the floor of the bedroom, he confessed telling her it was only that one time. "Kurt, I do not know you-you have changed, and this is not what I want for my life. I would like you to come home with me and let us begin our life together as we planned."

Kurt looked at her and for a minute he said nothing and then "Ava this is going to be my life from now on and if you cannot accept that this is what I want then we no longer have anything together."

Ava was devastated tears began to flow down her cheeks and she asked him "I thought we were in love and for years we had talked about and dreamed about what our lives would be what happened? Are you going to throw it all away for a thirteen-week gig in New York!" Now the tears were really coming down as Ava sat down on the chair.

"Don't you understand Ava I am successful. People love me. I am writing my own material. I have a chance to be very successful- with or without you. I want this opportunity; the life it affords because I love show business.

Either jump on the wagon or understand that this is going to be my life now. I will not change my mind. If you can't understand why then I will give you a divorce." Ava was stunned she picked up her bag and walked toward the door. "Once I walk out that door Kurt I will never come back in, and you will be out of my life do you want that-do you want me to be out of your life forever?" Her face searched for a sign of man she loved. She looked into his eyes but saw a cold stare.

Instead of love he responded "This may be the best thing that has happened to us Ava because I don't want a house full of kids or all that family stuff. I want this kind of success I want to be a star forever. You will never be able to share it with me. That is just too bad." Ava stared at him-he had a blank look on his face-not one of love, or fear of losing her." She turned opened the door and walked out. *who is this man she thought.*

She walked slowly to the elevator hoping for the man she loved to change his mind and come running out to stop her. But instead, he closed the hotel room door behind her without saying a word. Her marriage was over, and it had barely begun.

She decided to stay in New York for a day or two. Tired from her trip she booked a room. She was given room number 623. Ava slept seven hours and woke up in time for dinner. She ordered a light dinner and went out for a walk. walking close to the club where Kurt was performing, she decided to catch his act. She took a seat in the back of the room where she felt sure he could not see her. While he was funny Ava did not think he was good enough to be more than a night club act. She left without seeing Kurt but she caught a glimpse of him kissing Susie just as he left the stage.

Back at the hotel she tried to book a flight home the next afternoon, but the lines were busy. Ava tormented herself—*all the years of their being together —making plans about their life together-- she would never have dreamed this would have happened.* Her life seemed on hold. All she wanted to do was to get home and rest.

She dialed the airport again, the person on the telephone mentioned the possibility of standby for the 2 PM flight. Ava agreed to try it and arrived at the airport about 12:30 PM.

She checked in early just in case there would be a large group of people told to standby. The airport was crowded, she was tired, hungry and irritable. After checking in at the gate Ava went looking for a place to pick up a bit of lunch.

The airport had a nice sandwich bar, not too crowded considering this was New York City; when it was her turn, she ordered a turkey on whole wheat with light mayo and lettuce; just as she was speaking with the clerk a man interrupted her "just for a moment" he said as he put his finger up. He asked the clerk "Please make two of whatever she just ordered and put them in separate bags. Thank you."

"Excuse me!" said Ava. The man turned and said "Hi, I am Martin Bartlett and I hate waiting in lines. You were ordering just what I like and was going to order. I thought it would be easier to just let the clerk make two at a time.

Please don't be cross-you are too attractive to put lines in your face." Ava was stunned.

She began to speak "Mr. Bartlett" but he interrupted and said, "Dr. Bartlett" She continued "Ok Dr. Bartlett you are rude!" "Listen here ---what is your name?" "Hum, Ava" she hesitated for a moment and then "Ava West" Martin noticed her wedding rings and said "Now Mrs. West keep your shirt on-I explained myself and if you were kind, you would agree that waiting in line in New York is a b- - - h and finding you ordering just what I wanted was luck. You would also agree that making two sandwiches at a time is easier for the girl and"

Just then the clerk returned with the sandwiches both were in the same bag. "That will be $18.89 sir." Martin handed the girl a $20.00 bill and told her to keep the change. He then took out his sandwich and handed Ava the bag with her sandwich. There you are my dear-none the worse for time-and paid for- have a good day."

Dr. Bartlett began walking away. She watched him and was going to yell something but there were so many people all around the deli she thought she had better just chalk it up.

It appears the pressure in New York puts stress on people to keep things moving. New York is such a small area with people-all who have great ideas and little time.

Ava was angry but with Dr. Bartlett walking away there was nothing to be said or done. She was lucky and just made it in time to get on board of the plane. *The flight was crowded why were they were all going to Clayton?* she thought

This was a big plane with three seats on the right side of the plane and two on the left side. The ticket person said a seat was reserved for me, but the plane was full. Her seat was on the left side of the plane, and she was assigned set 22 B. When she arrived, she said "Oh NO! You, again!" Dr. Bartlett was in seat 22A. just then the flight attendant asked her to be seated for takeoff.

Dr. Bartlett said, "were destined to meet and talk." "Ok doc we met but we are not destined to talk." Ava sat down and the plane rolled down the runway. Dr. Bartlett began, "Mrs. West you need not be afraid of me-I know you think me rude-but you see I had a terrible night last night. My room at the Sheridan Hotel was given to another person because my business appointment kept me out until quite late. My secretary did not have a late arrival guarantee. I also understood from the hotel clerk that my room-was given to a very distraught woman, so I slept in the hotel lobby all evening. Then, to continue this ridiculous experience my luggage –was put in storage--at the hotel. When my room was given up, they could not find my luggage. Finally-you were ordering my favorite sandwich and I did not have any breakfast. So, you see Mrs. West I am not rude just had a miserable experience and did not sleep well and was hungry. I implore you to take pity on my rude behavior."

Ava was laughing and Dr. Bartlett said, "So you think my frustration and hunger is funny?" Ava could not contain herself "Well Dr. Bartlett, what was your room number?" "623" He answered. "Well Dr. I am the distraught woman who slept in room 623 last night at the Sheridan Hotel. Please do not call me Mrs. West—my name is Ava." "So, you're the lady that took my room may I ask what you were distraught about?" He said, "Well doctor let's just say I had a problem and leave it at that. Well then Mrs. West did you sleep well?" He asked.

"Yes, and it is not Mrs. West. Soon it will be Miss" she answered. "Oh, I am sorry." He answered. And just then the flight attendant was over asking about drinks. There was little time for discussion the flight was short, and landing was a couple of minutes away.

Ava was curious "Where are you from Dr. Bartlett? I mean you have a distinct accent. Is it British?" "Actually, I am French born in Quebec," he replied. "Are you staying in Clayton Dr.?" "No Ava, I'll be returning to Quebec. I am anxious to get home and see my two-year-old daughter who stays with my mother when I travel. My wife died a year ago." "Now, I am so sorry." Ava said. "Thank you, Ava" He answered.

The plane just landed, and everyone began assembling their luggage and moving down the aisles. "What is her name?" Ava asked. "Whose name?" He replied. "Your daughter's." Ava said. "Kayla Marie" he said. And with that the two of them walked into the airport. "I will be getting a rental car" Dr. Bartlett said. "Could I drop you someplace?" "No" said Ava. "My car is parked at the airport." "Then let me say it was very nice to meet you Ava and I could not have given up my room to a prettier person." Thank you" Ava said.

With that they shuck hands, and both went their separate ways. Since Ava did not have any checked luggage, she went to get her car. All the time she kept thinking how funny it was that she was the person who received his room. I suppose we were destined to meet.

BOOK 1111

Chapter 44

Surprises

Greta returned from Europe and learned that Ava was divorcing Kurt. She would be returning to France for a special assignment in a couple of weeks. She asked Ava to come join her. Ava said, "I am just not in the mood to travel. How long will you be gone this time mother?" Ava asked. "About two months." Greta replied, "This is a special assignment about French women. staying so thin-The world wants to know how the do it. This is a terrific opportunity for a United Press byline. I loved the idea and chose the assignment. Are you ok honey or do you need me to stay home for a while?" Greta was getting worried about Ava.

She understood going through a divorce is very distressful and she did not want to leave her emotionally struggling. "No mother I am fine. I am back to work, and I have already filed for divorce. I must wait to learn if Kurt is contesting." Ava answered.

"This whole thing must have really been hard. I am so sorry Ava-Kurt never seemed like the type." Greta was shocked at all the things her daughter had relayed. *She knew that Ava had a pipe dream about --Living Happily Ever After—but it was never Greta's dream.* Greta asked Ava to take her to the airport and she agreed.

Their visit was short-less than three weeks, but the two women had lived together for years and got along without issue. On the way to the airport Greta discussed how much she loved France and that she was taking an apartment. She asked Ava to visit. Ava assured her mother she was OK, and she would look for a week in her schedule to join her for a short vacation in France.

Ava left Greta and the entrance to American Airlines and the two women parted. As Ava drove away suddenly the feeling of true loneliness grabbed her. An English major in college *Ava thoughts encompassed the possibility of becoming a reporter like her mother. The only reason she became a teacher was because Kurt thought it was better to have summers off.*

All the way home she kept thinking of writing. Still in her younger days all she and her mother did was travel Ava could not phantom living out of a suitcase for a living. She understood her mother made good investments for her with her father's estate. She realized she did not need to work, she had money.

But...

Arriving back home Ava found herself back in the spare bedroom pulling out the journals saved by members of her family. She opened "Number 7." The title read: "This is a journal about Rita, and it had her letters to the family falling out of the book. The beginning pages were about how she and her husband met and the birth of Shana. The letters began in 1962.

The First one was February 16th.

"My Dear Betty,

I was amazed at my husband and all the things he had arranged for our move to Chicago. When we arrived, the new house was finished being painted, the repairs were completed, and our furniture set in place by an associate of Carl's named Margaret Powers. Ms. Powers had a car available on our arrival and listen to this:

She even arranged for a Chef to come to our new house and cook our first meal. Like everything else Margaret did- it was a perfect meal—delicious, and the chef was delightful. Margaret has a little boy-Joseph- he is blind. She lives with her father and son. She is a Viet Nam widow.

She arranged a personal banker for me to see and open our accounts. She provided me a bus schedule with a map. She completed the paperwork to enroll Shana in school.

The hospital Carl will be working for gave me a gift certificate to be used at their shop for $200; and gave Shana the same. And to top off all of this she bought a bedroom spread and drapes for a Shana in pink and purple. Shana loves her room. I just cannot say enough about how efficient Margaret has been. This move has been made quite easy.

On a different note, Margaret has arranged interviews for me at local schools. Say a prayer. Getting back to work would help me. with this move. Chicago is quite a busy city. Margaret says we are fortunate to live on what is called: "The Magnificent Mile." I cannot wait for all of you to visit. There are so many stores in walking distance -- not to mention great restaurants. We are close to the hospital and Carl could be home for lunch if he wanted. Well, that is it for now. Give my love to Dad. I really miss everyone already; I cannot wait for you to be here.

Love you all Rita"

Ava put the journal down thinking how fortunate Aunt Rita was to have a man that looked after her and thought of everything. She fell asleep in the bedroom. She must have been asleep for hours because it was dark when she woke up and the telephone was ringing. Greta's flight arrived in San Diego early. Her connective flight would be forty-five minutes late. Greta just wanted to "hear Ava's voice." The two women talked for about ten minutes when Greta's plane was called. Ava agreed to go to France for a week so they could be together.

After their conversation Ava was starved, she went into the kitchen for something to eat and just as she opened the refrigerator door the telephone rang again. It was her attorney Douglas Blancher he asked if she had heard from Kurt. she said she had not he said, "Ava you will and when you do call me immediately." Doug said. He sounded strange like concerned about something. She assured him she would call him. They talked, and Ava told him about her plans of going to France to join her mother for a week. He told her just to "keep in touch."

Three weeks went by, and Ava was still quite lonely and praying that Kurt would come to his senses and beg her forgiveness. But that did not happen.

She made plans to join her mother in France and even pondered quitting her job and staying in France until her mother's assignment was completed. The doorbell rang.

It was the post man asking her to sign for a registered letter from Kurt.

Chapter 45

Mommie

She opened the letter, and it began; "I will sign the divorce papers for 50% of your trust fund. If not willing, I will have to sue you!" Ava began to cry and picked up the telephone and called her attorney. He was in court. She then called Greta.

Unfortunately, the plane would not arrive in France for another six hours.

Greta fell asleep crying. The next morning, she tried to call Greta. Getting a telephone line to France took about fifteen minutes. When Greta heard about Kurt's threat, she told Ava not to worry-there is no way Kurt could get any of her estate. That was all Ava needed the next call she made was to quit her job. She walked around the house for an hour and then Douglas called. He told her he felt sure Kurt could not get any money from the estate, but he would call Mr. Cantor.

Finally, Ava thought *I need to get away. She called the airport and book the next flight to France. She packed only a small bag.*

The flight to France was tiring but when Ava arrived, she saw how beautiful her mother looked. "This country does wonders for you Mom" she said. Ava was so excited to see her mother she forgot all about Kurt and the letter. The ladies went ahead to the waiting cab and once inside they spoke about dinner. In the cab Greta spoke French and asked the driver for a restaurant that had a special cuisine she knew Ava would love.

Even though Ava and her mother had been in France together several times in years past Ava always marveled at how well her mother spoke French and knew her around.

The restaurant was small and quaint. The pictures on the wall were of girls. The name was "Mulan's" Greta chose a beautiful place. Once seated as always Greta proceed to tell the waiter their order: "Soupe Auc Carottes et Aux Lentilles; Moules a la tomate, salad du gourmet; cotelettes d`agneaw marinees a li orange et au gingembre and for desert yaourt glace a `La mangue." The meal was exquisite. The ladies left quite satisfied. Greta remarked that there is a show at the restaurant performed there every evening. But we will see it tomorrow.

At Greta's apartment the two women sat down with a glass of wine; Ava then told Greta all the details of the divorce. To her surprise Ava was handed a yellow envelope. In the envelope was a letter written by a woman named "Mildred Novelle. She was a student in the class that Kurt took during night school and the letter was written to Greta. It was opened and the body of it read:

"Dear Mrs. West,

I am Mrs. Miller's great granddaughter; I believe you and your family all knew my mother. Your son in law Kurt is currently in my acting class. He has not been doing your daughter any favors telling everyone in the class that she and you are millionaires. He says he married "Well." He is a flirt—I mean he has a reputation for kissing and hugging other women. If my daughter had such a husband –I would want her to know how he has been talking about her and her mother. I do not feel this is a loving husband!"

The next was a letter from Rennie Kenwick "I understand madam, I will hire Kurt for this club." Ava was devastated "Mom, did you set him up!" she screamed. "How could you?" Greta was firm "Ava once Kurt heard about your money-everything changed, and he changed. He came to my house and demanded I turn over all papers and pinpoint exactly what you had coming. He threatened me with a lawyer and when you were pregnant, he said he would have to protect his child. I did not arrange a twelve-week gig offer-that happened on its own. I just arranged one week. Rennie called me after the first night and said he was a success and thanked me for the "tip."

The next paper Ava was handed was from an attorney in Illinois assuring Greta that the trust was solid, and Kurt would not be able to touch it at all. Mr. Cantor had set up the estate of Slade West to protect Greta and the Baby from anyone who would try to capitalize of their holdings.

The evening was somber, the women found peace in each other. Ava wondered if her relationship for Kurt was based on a real love or just a young girl head over heels in love with love.

Ava asked Greta if at any time she had mentioned to Kurt the estate. She was relieved to know she had not. However, Greta said to Ava Kurt came to me the day after you told him about it.

Chapter 46

Regret and Love

Ava had a friend in Clayton who she asked to close her house. She planned to stay in France with Greta for the next two months. Greta was overjoyed; she was determined to make her daughter's stay special.

Christmas in France is beautiful. Greta saw to it that her daughter was lavished with gifts-all beautifully placed under a marvelously decorated tree in their apartment. While the women were out shopping, Greta hired a professional decorating company hired to come in on Christmas Eve while Ava was asleep and set everything up. It was just breath-taking. Greta told Ava they had to leave for-breakfast at 8 AM.

When Ava came down to leave for breakfast, she was stunned. The apartment was beautifully decorated with a tree and lights and wrapped presents. Greta arranged for breakfast to be served by a private Chef in their apartment with a table set and looking at the tree and beautifully wrapped gifts. Everything was ready and delicious.

After breakfast, Ava went to her room and brought down three gifts for her mother: a new shawl, a purse and a Christian Dior two-piece camel color suit. There were nine gifts under the tree for Ava: a new watch, two matching prints, an everyday 14 K gold Ruby ring, a new pair of sunglasses, a small statue of an angel, a teddy bear, a pair of slippers, a book with the authors signature, tickets to a special New Year's Eve gala being held by Greta's magazine. Ava was happy. Greta was doing everything she could to take Ava's mind off Kurt and the divorce.

The New Year's Eve gala was a special. Greta's magazine group rented the entire Mulan restaurant. There theater group would perform, and dinner was catered for the private showing of a New York musical. The performance was for Bye, Bye Birdie." After the show there was a party and a dance.

Ava noticed a man at the party watching them. "Mother who is the man standing in the corner of the room on the right? He has been watching us all night." Greta looked over and laughed. "That is Marcel" and with that she took her daughter's arm and the women walked over to the right of the room. "Marcel have you been staring at us?" Greta asked, "Wee madam, you and your daughter together are a vision of loveliness." "Ava" Greta said, "This is Marcel he is our security for the evening but during the day he is my friend and camera man." Greta asked if his wife had arrived yet and just as she did Carrie came over and gave them all a hug and kiss. Carrie, Marcel's wife, was 6 months very pregnant with twins. She was a lovely woman about 5'4" tall with big brown eyes and beautiful golden-brown hair. Marcel was obviously very much in love as he kissed her and held her hand as Greta introduced her to Ava. They were anxiously waiting for their first babies; Marcel touched his wife's stomach and said, "Daddy's here."

Just them Ava turned to a tap on her shoulder-as she turned there was Dr. Bartlett standing behind her. "May I presume you have something to do with this group?" He asked, "No" answered Ava-as Greta said, "Have you two met?" Ava was stunned that her mother new him. *Ava wondered what he was doing in France let alone at the same New Year's Eve dinner, show and party she was at.* Greta interrupted her thinking "Ava, Dr. Martin Bartlett is one of the sponsors of the article I am doing. His company owns the clinic here in France that I am writing about. Where did you too meet?" Before Ava could say anything, Dr. Bartlett answered "We met at the airport in New York, your daughter was kind enough to allow me to invade her space. We were also on the same plane back to Clayton. You have a most beautiful daughter Greta."

He turned to Ava and asked, "Ms. West they are playing "our song" may I have the pleasure of this dance?" With that Dr. Bartlett took her hand and they went ahead to the dance floor. "You look very beautiful Miss West" "Thank you Dr. Bartlett" "Please call me Martin" "Alright please call me Ava." The entire rest of the evening Martin Bartlett joined them at their table. He and Ava shared four dances out of the five that was played.

When the party was over Martin dropped them off at Greta's apartment.

Greta asked "Ava-he called you Miss West-why?" "It is a long story mom, as he said we met when I was leaving New York. I was devastated about Kurt. I did not want to explain everything to a stranger knowing I was filing for divorce. So, I just decided to use my maiden name." Greta liked Martin Bartlett *and she allowed her mind to explore the possibility of match with Ava. Still knowing Martin as she did, he would not leave Canada.* When the trip was over Ava was glad to be home. France was always one of her loves especially now that home-was different.

Chapter 47

Too Late

The next few weeks her attorney called every day. Kurt was frustrated, his attorney has told him there is no way he could touch Ava's holdings. He was asking for $250,000 in cash. Her attorney asked Ava would your mother agree to give it to him if he agrees to sign a paper yielding this is a final settlement. Ava flipped out "who is getting this divorce me or my mother!" but a second after she said that she apologized. She thought *I know my mother would just try to protect me and do it.* "I suppose she would, but I will not ask her to give it to him I want my attorney to manage it for now; Doug, please continue to try."

Four days went bye and Ava continued to ask herself *"Why she did not see this side of Kurt before?* She kept thinking *"I thought he was the love of my life-my heart. How could he play this game with me?"*

It was the first of February when her attorney called her again.

"Ava, I hate to give you this news, but Kurt's attorney now says they want $300,000 plus his attorney fees before he would sign the papers. I told him that was not possible, but he said that he would refuse to give you the divorce. What do you want to do?"

Ava was shocked and angry "You know what Doug, tell him that it is no deal. Tell him, I refuse to give him any money. I am changing my papers claiming abandonment, adultery, mental cruelty and blackmail. Tell him I am suing him for support and alimony. And I intend to have his wages garnished. Do not forget to add that I met Susie at the hotel. Add that the newspapers would love the story, and if the papers are not signed in five days, she will call the papers in New York."

Her attorney suggested "She is giving him five days to sign the papers-without any money was perfect. She agreed. She asked her attorney to tell Kurt she had an appointment to give an interview of Friday and she plans to mention how he left her and when she had miscarriages. She would also tell them how to find Susie." He said "I suppose you plan to mention that he demanded money before he would divorce you. I do not think this will hurt his career much, but it may hurt his ego." "Will do" Ava said, He attorney ended by saying "I think you will hear from him." It took less than a week and Kurt signed the papers.

Now Ava just needed to wait until it was all finalized, and she would be free. *Her heart was in pain-they went together for six years-and she never suspected this was a side of him. The agony was terrible. She lost five pounds in the first four days waiting for him to sign the papers. She could not sleep or go back to work for a week. Thank heaven that her boss did not believe she was going to quit, and he held her job for weeks.* Her attorney called two days later -it had been eleven months since the divorce began, he said today it was final! Knowing it was final Ava was depressed.

Chapter 48

Life is Full of Surprises

Even Greta's return home could not cheer her up. Summer was a blessing. Greta arranged for them to spend two weeks in Rome and another two weeks in France. Greta's article on the clinic was published and syndicated through the New York Times. She was up for an award. Her next assignment was in Germany, and she wanted Ava to join her. Ava said she would think on it but with just arriving home Ava needed some time.

When the two women were sitting in Ava's living room when Ava mentioned the journals to her mother. "I never heard of journals going all the way back to your grand-father's first wife-but Grandma Betty said something about a legacy that was left. That was what she was referring to. May I see one or two of them?" the ladies went ahead to the spare bedroom and the box of journals. Greta opened one that was dated 1952. The first thing in the box was a card to Rita:

"Rita, I am so happy I have a daughter. I wish it for you one day. She is the most precious thing I could behold, and she is mine!

Michael insists she be named Greta. He said it had something to do with a woman in Germany. I am not sure why he tells me he saw her less than three minutes before she was killed. He said he owed it to her to give her life and love.

Rita something happened to my husband in the war that changed him. He said this little girl and I mean the world to him that makes me happy. She will grow up to know how much she means to both of us. I hope you enjoyed my surprise-I know how much you love banana cinnamon bread. Love, Nora"

Greta was in tears. Her relationship with her father was strained to say the least. Then Greta read Betty's addition to the writing.

This was in one of Rita's bags of garbage when she stayed with me. I felt it should be added to the journals. Soldiers in Germany were warned about snipers, and Hitler sympathizers. It appears, four soldiers were scouting two in front and two in the rear. A brief time after they began their walk a woman appeared, it looked like she was holding a child or "so-it appeared" but it was a riffle. The women shot and killed three American soldiers before she was killed. Michael and I were out scouting Michael was a head of me and there was a woman with what appeared a child in her arms walking toward Michael. Because of losing three men just an hour before; I ordered Michael to shoot. He did not at first, but I ordered him to shoot again. As the woman got closer for the third time, I ordered Michael to shoot. When he did, he learned that the women really had a child in her arms and not a weapon. He never forgave himself. It was something that changed and haunted him, and I believe still haunts him and will for all his life."

Greta put the book down and cried. Ava tried to talk to her, but Greta waved her hand that she was not ready to discuss her tears with her daughter. The telephone rang and Ava left the room. Greta heard Ava upset on the telephone and she composed herself and went to see who was on the telephone.

Chapter 49

Regret

Low and behold Ava was talking with Kurt. Ava packed all Kurt's belongings when she filed for divorce. She sent everything to New York City to the apartment Kurt had rented.

Now, of all things, Kurt was asking Ava to allow him to return. He needed a rest and wanted to "come home." Ava said it was over and this was no longer his home, but he persisted. Begging for only a couple of days-he would stay in the guest bedroom. After about twenty minutes on the telephone Ava agreed to let him stay in the guest bedroom for three days.

When she was off the telephone her tears were flowing. Greta asked "Why let him come. You have been divorced more than a year and a half. He has been a bastard since he learned of your inheritance and even tried to get it as part of the divorce."

"I am not sure Mom. He sounded desperate and not really like himself. He was crying and …. I don't…I don't know why but possibly love does not die it just hides… maybe I feel sorry for him …maybe I am a fool who knows but three days is really nothing. He will be here Saturday. Let's get something to eat, I am starved."

Chapter 50

Wish I Knew

Kurt was arriving today, Ava was nervous. She told Kurt she would not be able to pick him up from the airport; he would have to take a cab to her house. When he arrived, he knocked on the door; when Ava opened it, she gasped! "Kurt, what happened to you!" she exclaimed. Her shock was in seeing Kurt thin, pale, his eyes with deep dark circles, he looked ill. "May I come in Ava?" He asked, "Oh my God-yes, yes, what sickness do you have?" Ava was in tears asking him. As Kurt came in Ava noticed he had difficulty walking and carried a cane. She helped him to the living room and to sit on the sofa.

He began "I am so sorry Ava for what happened. I was full of myself. I spent my life always being the one in the background, never having many friends. It was all the attention that came, and people liked my jokes. Then there was a beautiful woman that entered my life and I felt very manly. I felt like someone because she loved me and had faith in me. I suppose it was like maybe when a woman feels she is deeply loved and adored.

You see, there is difference; even though a person has the attention of a beautiful woman like you; when others recognize them, self-satisfaction enters and that is where recognition comes in. In my case that recognition was the applause, the publicity, and the fans, oh yes, the fans--it all changed me, as it has so many others."

You have not answered my question Kurt, "What is wrong?"

Kurt looked at her, lovingly touched her hand said "Ava I have stage four cancer of the esophagus. A lot of fame brings parties, dinners, liquor, drugs and a combination of pills, uppers and downers, not to mention the smoking many things and snorting. It all happened so fast.

One night there was this party with a group of people who stayed after the show. They were all friends of the owner and Susie. Of course, I was invited there after the show. It wasn't the first time at a party but eventually men brought in various kinds of drugs. Liquor was flowing first and of course we all sit around drinking and tired. Then a few people were using some drugs. I was leery at first but, with a few more parties, and more drinks, came the day I decided to try just one type of drug one e-leads to then another –and another and another.

I did not anticipate not be able to handle it until I woke up on the way to a hospital extremely ill. I passed out just as I was about to go on stage. I was in the hospital for two weeks. While there, I had a heart attack, some tests pointed to a hole in my esophagus. Further tests identified stage four cancer. That was two months ago. The doctor gave me "maybe" three months to live at that time. I did not want to bother you; I was terrible to you. Yet, you were the one I wanted, trusted and called. I remembered us, and how lonely my heart felt for someone who loved me all the time and not just my act. I should try to call the one person who genuinely cared about me—that was you, Ava.

I never loved Susie–she was an attentive person on my arm and there all the time. My ego was always being satisfied-but as for love—no not her. Ava, you have always been the one I love since the very first time I held you in my arms. I cannot perform any more. I am sick and dying. I just wanted to be near you again. May I stay here? It will not be for long. Ava I needed to tell you how sorry I am. How much of a fool I have been this past year."

Ava believed none of it and said, "What makes you think that all people, including those others in show business do not feel the same as you described? Those that live their life in balance and do not put too much emphasis on applause, keep a conscious awareness as to where their recognition comes from; and how to appreciate it by respecting their fame channeling it for good, keeping their senses about them. Of course, all people are vulnerable to liquor, drugs, and the love of recognition-it takes focus and determination not to let those things take a road to eventual destruction.

Ava was in tears. All the love she had so successfully buried in years now appeared for Kurt.it was her first realization that love does not die; it hides in the subconscious to be able to go on with life, after a death, or after a divorce, really after any loss.

When something brings it forward it is as if it never left. Ava loved Kurt-was terribly hurt by his greed, lust, meanness, and lying.

But all that said and done, now—Kurt needed her. His presence brought back the feelings that were so successfully hidden. "Yes, Kurt you can stay here. I will take care of you, she said. Let's get you into the guest bedroom you look tired from your trip."

All he could say was "Thank you Ava" and with that she helped him to the room and then undressed him and put him in bed. He was asleep in a matter of minutes. Ava just looked at him for a minute. *Her thoughts went wild from anger to love.*

Chapter 51

Changing

It was about 8 PM when Greta returned from her party. She was leaving in two days for Chicago to visit Rita, Katherine, and JC, and then off to Germany for six weeks. When Greta checked in, with Ava and herd about Kurt, she was shocked. "I will stay home for few days we will both take care of Kurt. I will try to help." Ava thanked her mother.

Ava decided Kurt should be seen by cancer specialist. Kurt slept through the night. Ava checked on him a couple of time-and he was still asleep. The next morning Ava made him breakfast; she mentioned his seeing a specialist here in Clayton. He argued, he had seen enough doctors in New York City, but he would do this just for her.

The doctor was terrific. Kurt had an appointment the next morning. Ava and Kurt spent a calm day together. But when Ava went to the grocery store, Kurt was alone with Greta. He told her he knew she was somehow involved in his getting the club offer. He said when he learned of Ava's inheritance, he had become greedy and behaved stupidly. He was sorry for that and for becoming a fool.

He told Greta, "You need to protect Ava from fools like me." and she agreed. Greta spent years watching her daughter and Kurt be in love. Greta told Kurt that "Everything Ava was to inherit would have helped make a good life for you too. I am sorry for the way things worked out; I hope the doctors in Clayton could save you. I will help you in any way I can."

"Greta, I never appreciated you, from our beginning you and Ava were close I envied that closeness. But that was what I loved-she was kind, considerate, respectful, logical, and loving of us both. You were always the one she wanted to emulate."

Chapter 52

Too Late

Kurt's meeting with the doctor was brief. The doctor suggested he be admitted for a couple of tests. They agreed. But the doctor asked to speak with Kurt alone; Ava and Greta left the room. The doctor told Kurt he would make him comfortable. Kurt thanked him and said it would be better for it to happen her here rather than in Ava's house with her alone. Kurt asked the doctor to call Ava after it was over, the doctor agreed. Kurt would be in the hospital a short time when he passes away. There was nothing they could do. It was not the cancer that killed him it was his heart-it just gave out, the doctor just relieved some of the pain.

Ava received a call at 4 AM when he went into cardiac arrest. It was over as fast as it began. He was in the hospital two days. Kurt's uncle divorced his second wife just after Christmas and died just a month before Kurt of lung cancer. He was a heavy smoker. After the divorce he went to see Kurt and he paid most of the medical bills Kurt had until there was nothing left.

It was up to Ava to take care of the arrangements. She began to pack Kurt's things and saw a letter addressed to her in one of bags. She opened it:

"My Dear Ava,

I never really appreciated you-and the love you offered me. I am sorry. It took this to realize I have always loved you. The first day I held you in my arms you gave me your trust and your heart. I did not value it then because I was a fool.

What happened to me is something I cannot explain. Your mother would call it greed-and she might be right. But it was more than greed-it was a feeling of not ever being in control. You had everything; I wanted you to look up to me instead of me feeling at the mercy of your mother, your personality and success and then your estate. Whatever it was it is too late to go back. I acted like a foolish child. But Ava, I learned that money really is not important, it is true LOVE, TRUST and FAMILY that brings richness more than money.

I did not recognize; I did not even know myself why I felt the way I did until I was in the hospital and a psychologist came into my room. We spoke off and on for a week.

I am sincerely sorry, I know I destroyed that starry eyed, faithful girl who put all her love and trust in me. Your heart must have been broken and you must have been deeply hurt by how I acted. I have been a fool. Everything I have-which is not much-is yours.

I realize your love was the best thing that could have happened to me. I saw an attorney and turned over the building I bought to you, and I have little left from the money that I took to build my business but that has been put in an account in your name.

Please try to forgive me-I wish you love, happiness and a new life without the pain I brought into your life.

I love you, Kurt."

There was a bank book in the envelope, and it was only in her name. There was $403,000 in the account left from 1.5 million.

That he kept in cash over the cost of the building.

Two days later Ava and Greta were on a plane to Arizona. They cremated Kurt, per his wishes and took the askes to Arizona. Kurt wanted to be buried next to his uncle in a private service. It was difficult saying goodbye to Kurt-again. Kurt was only twenty-seven years old, when he died. A life taken so young seems a waste.

Ava swore to herself she would never love or trust anyone like that again. Kurt, their marriage and his death had taken from her that unassuming starry-eyed vision of life and no matter what she would never allow it to return.

Chapter 53

A Surprise

Greta left for Chicago when Ava went to Arizona. She had a schedule to adhere to and still had to be in Germany by August 1st. She would shorten her time in Chicago visiting with family. She invited Ava to join her in Germany, but Ava wanted to stay home for a while.

Ava decided to rent her house and move back in with Greta, a move that delighted Greta. It took her two months to sell her furniture and move what was left into Greta's basement. She put an ad in the paper and a young woman called. Her brother had a position at the Clayton hospital, he was a doctor, and she would be moving with him. Ava met them and showed them the house. They loved it and wanted to rent with an "option" to buy if she ever decided to sell. Ava agreed.

Chapter 54

Knowledge

With Kurt gone and Greta in Germany for another month; it was a time for reflection and rest. Ava was tired, confused, frustrated, lonely and angry all at the same time.

It did not take long, and she found herself back in the room with the journals. She picked up one without reference to date or time and opened it. Then was something that fell out. It was a letter.

A letter addressed to "Ava West." She recognized the writing as Great Grandma Betty's, and she opened it and began to read:

"My Dear Ava,

I knew if I left you this house and said you had to live in it for at least a year you would find the journals and this letter. I love you Ava very much. These journals give you roots to your mother's family. I only wish I could have done the same for your father's.

Greta told the family little about your dad. None of the family every met him. So, your Great Grandma Betty thought it would be important for you to have a bit of grounding. This is what I knew. We were not allowed to discuss your father with Greta or you. All we really knew was that they never married, and he left you and her everything he had. There was a secret-but never mentioned.

These journals go back to when Great Grandpa Kevin was married to his first wife. She must have been a lovey woman. Your great grandfather was a different man with her-someone I wished I knew him at that time. I wish I had met him first. Our lives would have turned out differently, as it is now, we live separately, he chose to move into a retirement home when we sold our house.

Lilly had a secret as well. She had a child out of wedlock. Her son wanted to meet her after his adoptive parents passed away. He located Lilly and his father. His father passed away in World War 11.

Lilly was living with Michael and Nora after she suffered a fall and her husband passed away. They all loved Christopher when he came to live with them.

Christopher renovated Michael's house and then because he had leukemia he passed away. What a terrible secret for Lilly to have all along most of her life. It was a different time.

I hope these journals help you to learn how life evolved for your family. I hope your life and love turns out better than any of ours.

As a child you used to say that one day you were going to be a famous writer. I think writing is in your blood like it is in your mother's. hopefully, these journals will help you get to be that famous writer

You are loved,
Great Grandma Betty"

Ava put the letter down and began to cry. She fell asleep on the bed and woke up to the telephone ringing. It was Greta she arrived safely in Chicago. "Mom, may I ask you something?" Ava said, "Always honey, are you sad about Kurt?" Greta answered. "No Mom, but I need more about my father, and I was just wondering who else you could, or would tell me more, would it be Mr. Cantor?" Ava said. "Ava, all you need to know is that your father was a decent man who loved you and me completely. He left you a legacy and died before you were born. I must go my cab is here-I am off to Germany. Please visit me. Love you." And with that she was gone.

Ava's curiosity was up, and she suddenly became determined to learn about her father. What was the secret Great Grandma mentioned? It was time I learned about Slade West-she thought.

I suppose there is only one other person I could ask questions to and that is Mr. Cantor and his doctor daughter Lisa. I will give them a call in the morning and book a plane to New York.

Chapter 55

Searching and Discovery

The last Four days had created a turn in Ava's life. There was a growing and creating a wall that she would not permit to quit.

It was still summer, and Ava called her mother in Chicago after she landed. She mentioned she just rented her house; was away on business but promised to visit her in Germany. Greta did not understand but was pleased that Ava planned to visit in her.

Then Ava brought out all the boxes of journals from the closet and began reading. Days went by and she would read most all day. Then she read a letter from her Grandmother Nora to Aunt Rita about her mother.

"It has been so long since Greta has called or come home.

I so wish that she and her father were on better terms..."

Ava read all about Michael cutting her mother's hair and what happened at the school. She read about Germany and her father killing the lady and her child during the war. There was the letter from her Grandfather's Army Sargent, and the letter from Michael to Nora on their 20th anniversary. It was so nice that they Betty and Charlie moved in together as they got older. Obviously, after Charlie's death Michael and Nora and Betty moved in together.

Then after a week of reading she came upon a note from her Grandmother Nora.

"Tell, me how Betty we are going to talk to this child about Slade West. Do we say she was conceived by a rape?"

Ava jumped up and put the books away. She could not read anymore. Her mother never mentioned that she was...conceived through a rape!? How? Ava wanted to know all the details and why her mother made out like her father was Saint!

Ava knew Slade West lived in New York; she was determined to learn all she could about him. She remembered Mr. Cantor and found his telephone number. His secretary made an appointment for her the next afternoon. On the telephone Ava said her married name "Connie Blitz." She booked a seat on a plane out that night and registered at the "Hilton" under the name "West."

That night all she could think about was why her mother did not every mention how she was raped? As Ava thought about the scenario, she decided that Greta just wanted to protect herself and Ava.

The next morning, she went to Mr. Cantor's office and his secretary said "They are waiting for you Ava, please go in." Ava thought who are "They? And how did she know it was me!" When the door opened Mr. Cantor was with another lady sitting in his office. He said, "Good morning, Ava. May I introduce my daughter Dr. Lisa Cantor." Ava said, "I do not understand, you all knew it was me--how?" "My secretary checked with the hotel; you were listed as Ms. West."

"Please sit down." Mr. Cantor said. "We know about you Ava; through the years your mother has always kept us informed. We knew, one day you would be coming to us with questions about your father. Ava, I was not just your father's attorney I –we--were all close friends of your father, for years, Lisa grew up calling him Uncle."

Ava was in the office with Dr. and Mr. Canton for over three hours. Mr. Cantor and his daughter spoke of how they met Slade West, the kind of jobs he had as an emergency medical technician, the property he had purchased, the house he built, and the tragic deaths of his daughter and his wife. They told Ava about the size of his estate when it was turned over to Greta; and how the sale and mortgage of the medical complex to his daughter and x-wife would increase her funds for years.

Then Mr. Cantor went to his safe. "Ava, your mother does not know about this—but your father left you a letter. Your mother was given two letters but this one was to be held here if you ever came looking for information about your father." The one thing not discussed or gone into detail was Slade's death. Dr. and Mr. Cantor both said his death was an accident.

With that statement Mr. Cantor took an envelope out of his safe and handed it to Ava. "This is now yours to take. Lisa and I do not know what is in the envelope." The words on the envelope were "Private for my unborn child" Ava thanked them both and left. She asked if they would agree to another appointment. Mr. Cantor said "Of course"

Once in her hotel, she *thought my mother must have been devastated when she found out she was pregnant, and my father was dead. But she kept me and loved me, and my father loved her and me. There is so much to think about.* She was tired and hungry. She placed the envelope in her suitcase and took a hot bath. After her bath she ordered room service then took a nap.

Rested she ordered a light dinner, and then decided it was time to read the letter from her father. She hesitated to open it, as she sipped her coffee, she just looked at the writing. She *thought* *"Well he had nice handwriting."* Finally, she opened the envelope and began to read:

"My Dear Child,

If you have this letter, it is because you are interested in knowing who your father was and the facts surrounding his meeting your mother and their having you. I have no doubt that your mother would not disclose all the facts of our time together. She is a jewel of a person, and it would not be in her nature to in any way dispel the image she created. I am confident that the image she has given you of me lacks something.

Make no doubt I loved your mother deeply. That is why I ..."

At this point Ava put down the paper. She had begun to cry. It was difficult to continue reading. She placed the letter back in the envelope and dialed Greta.

Ava called Greta. She did not tell her mother she was going to New York; she began their conversation with exchanging pleasantries. "Hello Mother, I miss you. How are you? How is Chicago.?" Greta knew her daughter very well. "I am fine dear. How are you? Have you had a good day?" Greta played along knowing full well that Ava was in New York, saw Dr. and Mr. Cantor and that she had an envelope from her father. Mr. Cantor called her when Ava left the appointment.

"Mother I want to tell you something" "Of course Ava, you know you could tell me anything." Greta answered. "Mom, I am in New York, I went to see Mr. Cantor." "Oh" said Greta. "You see Mom I read something in the journals, and I wanted to see if it was true." Ava said. "Why didn't you just ask me honey, and save yourself time?" Greta asked. "Because I did not think you would tell me---u--e would tell—u--truth." Greta gasped, "Ava I do not lie to you. You should know that by know. What is your question?"

"Mom, how was I conceived?" Ava asked. "Well honey, it is a long story but the crux of it is your father was a widower for many years, when something happened that I was not able to participate in our love making he –he— he still made love to me." Greta paused-after all these years she could not call Slade West rapist. "Mom did my father rape you?" Ava asked.

Greta watched her words carefully "Ava, I was falling in love with your father. We would have made you together, but time did not allow. When your father made love to me, I was not feeling well, and he went ahead.

There are those who would have called it a rape, but I do not."

Greta knew that Dr. and Mr. Cantor did not tell Ava it was a rape, nor did they tell Ava how her father died. Ava has always heard it was an accident. "Mom, I feel I am missing something-like there is some secret I am not being told and it hurts. I am a big girl, married, cheated on and divorce. I can take it." Ava said pleading with her mother. Greta refused to be bullied or tormented into raking Slade West over the coals. "Ava" she said firmly "Ava your father was a decent man and he loved both of us very much. I will not let you believe that someone's poor choice of words defines him. I loved him and I love you-that is all that matters!"

That is when Ava interrupted, "Mom I have an envelope here with letters to me written by my father." "Yes" Greta answered, "Am I to presume your father said her raped me?" she asked. "I am not sure Mom I have not read everything yet. But I really wanted to hear things from you." Ava said. "How did my father die?" since Greta did not know for sure how Slade died, she merely repeated what she had been told. "It was an accident. That is what I have been told all these years and that is what I told you." Now Greta needed to leave for an appointment. "We can continue this when you call again if you need more information." And with that Greta said goodbye.

Ava was more determined than ever to find out how her father died. She opened the envelope once again and pulled out all the papers.

"Make no doubt I loved your mother deeply and I know she loved me. She is a fine upstanding woman with principles. Do you know how hard that is to find? When your mother had an accident with her car, I put her to bed. She is so beautiful I could not just stop myself from making love to her. She is a kind, gentle and intelligent woman. I am positive she will tell you that we were falling in love.

Men have other issues when love is involved and sometimes, we let those issues be decided first. Pay no mind-to that your mother and I were in love as sure as I am writing this, I know she loves you very much.

I hoped you would like to see your family tree, so I am enclosing a few pictures. There fist picture is of my wife she died five years before I met your mother. The next one is of our only daughter she died too young. I am also enclosing pictures of myself-figuring you may want to see what I looked like over the years. The last album of pictures is of the house I built. I am also a good cook. I hope my cooking talent rubs off on your enjoyment of cooking."

Ava put the envelope down. There is no mention of a rape or anything about how she was conceived. All that was left in the envelope was more pictures and a final sentence.

"I would give anything to be there with you and be able to hold you in my arms. I love you and your mother with all my heart."

Love,
Dad

Ava felt depressed. Somehow, she would find out how her father died. She dialed Mr. Cantor's office and tried to make an appointment for the next morning. Mr. Cantor's secretary said he was leaving for vacation tomorrow, but he is in the office now and available to speak with her. When Mr. Cantor was on the telephone Ava asked, "Please tell me how my father died?" Mr. Cantor answered "Ava your father had an appointment with a friend. The friend was to meet him at his house. When the person arrived, he went into the house, as your father rarely locked the door if he was home. The friend found him dead on the floor dead. It was quite a shock and he called me at once." "From what did he die of Mr. Cantor?

A man does not just die and there is no autopsy or medical report I checked?" Ava was now in tears and her voice very demanding.

"Ava, your father knew it was just a matter of time and he was going to die. My daughter is a doctor-your father had heart issues through the years, he was on medicine for a long time. My daughter signed the death certificate. It reads Heart Failure," Mr. Cantor said. Ava was not satisfied; she wanted more information. "May I call your daughter?" Ava asked.

Now, Mr. Cantor realized it would not be a good situation if Ava called Lisa; so, he went one step further. "Ava, you need to put this to rest. Your father was stressed, he lived through challenging times, with a torn heart, the deaths of his daughter and then his wife. He tried to keep fit but he knew his life was going to be short. Digging up information about his health and medicine will not change the fact, Ava; he is dead. The important things are that he loved you and your mother. He left you both everything he had; your mother has been careful about spending all these years. She has a life estate from your father's holdings. The sale of the medical center was recently made; that is the beginning of transfers to your estate until you reach thirty. Then, every five years more passes to you until your mother's death. At this time, thanks to your mothers' business savvy, the estate has more than tripled since your father's passing. You and your future families are set for life. Continuing to dig up stuff will never satisfy all your questions. I am confident your mother will help you fill in the blanks."

With that, the conversation was over; Mr. Cantor said he had another call he needed to take. Mr. Cantor and his daughter

Lisa agreed with Greta years prior never to use the word "suicide or rape." They all agreed on the story to tell Ava all her life. Before Ava left New York she decided to see her if she could look up the newspaper death notices of her father's death. The only thing she could find was the date of his death and the fact that he was cremated. It was a disappointment but now it was time to return to Clayton.

Once back in Clayton Ava decided to continue reading the journals. Three days of rest went by and now she was pulling out the box marked Rita.

Chapter 56

Rita

She got to the point of where Aunt Rita met Uncle Carl and the telephone rang. It was Edward Stevens an old college acquaintance. He heard Ava was a widow and he wanted to help in any way he could. Edward Stevens was living in Chicago just completing his education at

Northwester Law School. He just learned about Kurt's death. He was getting married soon. He suggested when Ava visits family in Chicago give him a call.

Ava promised to look him when she was in Chicago. He gave her his address and telephone number. She put it aside; she was not in the mood for seeing anyone.

Her whole life was before her --H*ow could all these things have happened? Her life was charmed, she had a beautiful childhood and then love with Kurt. Why would these things happen money destroyed Kurt. When he found out about the inheritance he wanted as much as he could get for himself. Money and fame both destroyed him and their marriage.* Ava decided to change her future—I can never marry again-my money will destroy it and it will destroy the man I would marry.

Ava dialed Greta. She arrived in Germany but mentioned that her next assignment was at the new clinic opening in Toronto. Greta had trained Ava to write like a reporter for years; she asked Ava to oversee the opening of Dr. Bartlett's new clinic. *Besides, she was also play-ing match make and that would be a good match.* Greta knew Dr. Bartlett for the last four years and felt he would be a good catch. She was not aware that he was already committed to a young woman in Canada.

Ava agreed to cover the opening. It would be in ten days, she made all the arrangements and let Dr. Bartlett know. He was overjoyed at the opportunity of meeting her again and having an article written on the new clinic.

Ava began preparations for the trip. She learned all she could about the good doctor's clinics; in doing so she learned about how he cared for his mother and put his sister through medical school. Dr. Bartlett's sister was married to a pastor and lived in Switzerland, doing research on identical twins.

Ava's was to be in Toronto in two days. Once again Ava sat down with a cup of coffee to read the journals.

"Kevin no longer loves me. I feel like a fool why do I love him the way I do? I pray for something to change. I realize nothing is perfect, but I thought we were in love. Kevin has been jealous for no reason just because I clean for John and Charlie. Now, I ask you how that indicates I like being with men. How stupid is that? Try to tell Kevin he is wrong; and you will realize he could not accept anyone saying he is wrong!

Ava put the book down. This page was all she needed to solidify building a wall in her mind and heart against love and marriage.

The drive to Toronto was pleasant. Ava found old tapes of Connie Francis and Frank Sinatra; she listened to them and sang with the tapes all the way to Toronto and the hotel. To her surprise there was a message from Dr. Bartlett—he was not going to be at the opening. The doctor left for Switzerland earlier in the week; his sister was in the hospital.

Dr. Bartlett left this message; "My sister suffered a fall and will be going into surgery on Friday. Mrs. Joyce Louise Moore will be the hostess at the opening. She is one of the major contributors for the clinic. She will be expecting you Ava."

Ava and Mrs. Moore hit it off perfectly. After the opening Mrs. Moore invited Ava to join her for dinner the next evening at a French restaurant. Dinner was great and two women were very compatible with never a lull in conversation during dinner. Mrs. Moore invited Ava to her summer home in the Hampton's at the end of August and Ava accepted.

There was a note for Ava from Dr. Bartlett apologizing for leaving her to others for the opening. He said in a few days he would be back in Toronto, if she had any questions.

Chapter 57

Changing

The article Ava wrote regarding the opening of the clinic in Toronto was excellent; Greta was proud of her daughter's article. Th paper loved all the pictures that accompanied the article, it solidified her receiving a byline.

The second week of July Ava visited her mother in Germany. They met Hans Glisson in Berlin. Hans sixty years old, custodian working at the same school for the last twenty years.

The school was not doing well as funding was denied. Currently there are only ten students and one teacher. Mr. Glisson asked Ava and her mother to draft an article in the hopes of finding those interested in helping the school financially. The ladies agreed. Greta and Ava promised to do their best in helping the school.

Chapter 58

Time

Time moves by quickly when you are busy; Ava always put her heart and soul into her writing. She wrote a note-turning down the opportunity to spent time with Mrs. Moore in the Hampton's asked for a rain check. Identifying her new assignments would be taking her out of the country for a while.

Ava was offered to author a series of articles on the different education systems in foreign countries. She agreed to author on five countries over the next year. Her agreement offered an option to continue for a second year if the articles generated much success.

It meant traveling a great deal, luckily her mother received a contract to work on articles of different holiday traditions in each of the same five countries. Greta and Ava spent Christmas and New Year's Day in New York City. The shops were especially beautifully decorated, but the ladies did little shopping. Hard to carry several bags to five countries.

The Macy's parade was great and had everyone on their toes waiting for Santa. The holidays gave her an opportunity to enjoy time without thinking or feeling lonely. Greta spoiled her child.

The Syndicated Press asked both Ava and Greta to run a regular column monthly of their experiences traveling to five countries for the paper. They agreed to do it alternately one of them at a time since the articles would be bylined.

Accepting the articles on travel, holidays and educational systems did not leave Ava and Greta time for anything else. With Greta deciding to join her and co-author her articles the ladies were becoming quite a pair in all the syndicated papers.

Greta *thought It might be interesting to author an article about togetherness as mother and daughter working, living and authoring articles together. She de-cided it would be better for a book one day after she retires.*

Chapter 59

Here We Go

The ladies decided their assignments should begin in Rome. This was the first time both mother and daughter would be accepting assignments in the same countries and alternating regular articles. Ava would write about the educational system. Greta would write about the festivities and the celebrations.

It was an opportunity made in heaven. The ladies decided to take some extra time for themselves in Rome between assignments. Their editor arranged for them to have an apartment for a period of three months all expenses paid.

Getting ready to leave for Rome; the plane departs in two weeks; was stressful packing for three months as it required considerable thought about the changes in the weather; also. their visit would overlap holiday festivities.

The Sunday prior to leaving Greta received a hysterical telephone call from Rita. Katherine needed surgery and Jeff and Carl were out of town; Rita needed Greta's help. Greta told Ava she would meet her in Rome as soon as she possible after she helped Rita and Katherine.

With Greta in Chicago Ava had time to herself before she had to leave for Rome. She decided to pack the journals into a storage box in her mother's basement.

She was thumbing through them looking, searching for something of substance—more than "we all had dinner...or it was a perfect Christmas." Betty had written about so many of those days; Ava would just pass on reading about the "great" dinners. She came to a section mentioning Rita and so she settled down and began to read.

"Rita and Carl have had problems for years. Even Carl delivering their twins did not seem to do much for their relationship. One would think that the delivery alone would have brought them closer. Their relationship is the topic of conversation every time the family gets together.

Kevin is upset. Michael says Carl does not appreciate the opportunities given him by having a loving wife and a close family. Rita argues that Carl is a Leader, a Developer and an Entrepreneur in his field. His focus was on developing a way of grafting skin to help burn patients survive and his burn cream would help them also live a normal life.

Rita reminded her family that Carl was always kind, respectful and helpful to all of them. Always taking care of miner health issues and giving advice along with providing them a laugh at his stories. Kevin said she was blindly in love with love and Carl knew just how to keep her that way. He was so upset with her last week visiting when she cut her vacation short and went home.

Kevin asked if she would ever divorce Carl and come home. She said "NO" emphatically "NO! because I have a home with my husband and children, and I do visit everyone here often. You are all welcome to visit us more often." Kevin's mind was made up-he thought *Carl took advantage of Rita from the beginning.*" Nora said, "like his feelings of Betty, my father's mind pulls him in strange directions and nothing and no one can change him."

As usual when I disagree with Kevin's thinking we do not talk for weeks. When Rita was beaten and raped by that lunatic Carl stayed with her all night in the hospital. He was there for her-taking her to see a counselor for the rape and he was there to help her buy her car. He used to be with her all the time until he hit on the different techniques for treating burn patients. Then not only did that not work well, but he developed a surgery and a burn cream that gives the patient a great chance and provides security for his family.

It was doing all this that they fell in love. He took the family to Chicago-to help the family have more security. Carl's operating methods for burn patients and his creams are unbelievably successful.

Yes, he needed to work long hours and he does travel a lot. But he stayed home when Rita was pregnant; luckily, he was there when she went into labor a month early. He delivered his own twins and arranged for an ambulance to take her to the hospital right after the birth.

I do not know what Kevin wants. He throws stones at everyone; he should examine his behavior in our relationship. He is anything but a loving husband these days.; the reason he gives is absolute stupidity.

Carl is a doctor with a successful idea; he needed to be where his idea became a reality? Rita has her own issues over the years, and she blindly refused to address them. She is always fearful of everything-that must be because of the rape."

Betty

Ava put the book down-she thought about the word "rape." Another one of my family was raped-how does this happen?

Aunt Rita is always trying to organize events. She is ridged in her feelings and dogmatic in what she felt was right. She was afraid of things happening out of her control-fear does such strange things to a person.

Ava did not know her aunt was raped. She wondered if Rita's feelings were due to what she endured with the rape. Uncle Carl always makes a joke about her ideas, saying her fear won out. She seems fearful about one thing or another. I wonder if the fear that develops-after a trauma changes a person's ability to trust anyone in the future. Ava decided to continue reading...

"I am really confused. I though love covered- all evils-but do we cover them at our own expense and live a lie? What do we do? It is hard to know just what is right.

Carl is good person and helpful according to Rita. He tries to be available when she or the children need him. Rita is insecure in herself, and she does try to please and take care of Carl.

Over the years, it is a fact that Carl really knows how to manage people; his key is understanding people's attitude, demeanor and language all together. Carl was not really close to his family in the past—they did not even know about the wedding or his move to Chicago. Michael said, "Rita has been there for all his ventures and for all his successes. She says her love is unconditional.

She once said "If Carl is committed to the marriage-whether there is a marriage, or companionship-I will stay with him. When you make a choice to love someone-you will need to understand that all relationships change over time. Nothing is perfect so you make mental and emotional commitments to keep dialogue open, understand, compromise, and forgive while continuing to love. Love is not feeling; a married person cannot be afraid that their mate will take advantage of them. The fact is that in many marriages one does take advantage." "I think, that is where I disagreed with her because I think a couple should be growing together to become one," Michael said.

Betty said she was thinking: *There are times I wish...Kevin and I continued to make love. He is the man I want to be with even if we are barely companions. Funny, I never thought I would say or feel something like this ever. I guess love must bear pain as well as joy. Just seeing him come in the house makes me happy. What a stupid silly woman I am! But physical closeness is keeping that relationship happier.*

Betty continued "When it comes to visiting Clayton-Rita comes alone these days and this makes Kevin angry. This last time, Carl took the children with him to visit his sister Carol. Kevin said "How does a man just shut-out his wife and grandparents. I wonder how this really will affect their children's relationships with mates in the future. Isn't a father supposed to set an example of how a man should treat his wife?" The children did come with Carl and Rita for Christmas and New Year's.

Ava put the book down her thoughts were running wild. *"Some people (I think mostly men) do have a problem with marriage. It is as if those (men) people want to stay single but still want the love of a good mate who will (For men: have their children) and not interfere with them. They do not seem to understand or realize that relationships change when marriage happens; marriage carries first and foremost a choice along with a personal responsibility of adjusting to pleasing another person, with compromise, setting good examples (especially when children come along), and becoming a team that no one could or would break. A true commitment to each other of understanding each' others faults and good points working together for the benefit of EACH OTHER. Children grow up and leave to begin their own households- a husband and wife are left with each other. If they have not bonded to that becoming one; they become lonely, selfish-feeling unloved and indifferent to their mate, still looking for happiness.*

And pray tell what is happiness--- if it isn't being loved, cared for, wanted, thought of, appreciated, there to share one's success and failures, to enjoy life together, someone who does things just to make you happy? Many marriages end in divorce only to find the same situations of dissatisfaction repeat itself. And if that becoming one does not happen in the second marriage one just keeps going looking for that certain someone. That is a waste of time, energy, money, emotions, and a loss of happiness.

That is not what should happen. If it does, what seems to grow in many relationships is one or the other finds "happiness" talking to strangers-telling them of their successes and dislikes-all while in the marriage.

It should be that parents-set out to be an example in front of the children working out their issues while becoming one-not in anger or arguments but in heartfelt conversation.

Yes, in a marriage the couple will need private conversations of heart—but compromise is part of that becoming one-understanding, forgiveness and acceptance are not just words—they are means of emotional and intellectual growth.

Ava thought: Except for George and Lilly, and Michael and Nora I do not know a married couple so much in love and really have become one-as in the bible?

That just re-affirms my feelings-I am not sure marriage is for me let alone another relationship. I will need to keep my firm resolve foremost in my mind and heart.

Ava did not realize it but her feelings and attitudes about love, men and marriage were building a large emotional and mental wall that would be difficult for any man to tear down.

It was a wall of protection—a protection for her heart, trust and for her emotions, and even for her money. The only way walls come down are with trust. She was determined not to trust any man again because her money or things would be what breaks that bond-so don't make the bond and you will not be disappointed or go through the pain...I will not marry again! Ava said out loud- ten times to build those words into her mind!

Many marriage vows include "In sickness and in health, in good and bad times, 'til death do you part." We say "Yes" to be engaged and "Yes" to be married. We do have a choice.

Before Ava's plane left for Rome, she called her mother in Chicago inquiring about Katherine. "The doctors think it is possibly ovarian cancer" Greta said. "When Carl heard he flew in to talk with the doctors and check out he x rays. We will know more in a day or two."

Again, Ava felt frustrated *"why would this happen to her cousin? She is married with two beautiful children. She has a loving husband; she never heard anything but happiness from Katherine. Although Katherine's relationship with her mother did leave something to be desired. Some of that is just the difficulty of lack of bonding.*

It seems working families spend little time just sitting and talking and playing games together and loving being together. Friends, television, words to music, movies, and now video games, along with the antics of Hollywood characters, story lines-- all appear to have more influence; as Life has become-taking kids to lessons-soccer, football, baseball, dance, music lessons, etc.

Discipline then becomes emotional-instead of discipline (it should never be harsh) why not try understanding: why we need rules and what is learned because of them—along with true appreciation, recognition and respect for the child. all that becomes is good communication.

It is too bad that schools do not begin from and early age to teach not just verbal words but instead the meaning of true recognition of how communication works. For example: how simple words such as: "you are" could be destructive if added to stupid, a retard, a reject, toxic, a weird-oh. Toxic communication destroys relationships because those words are hard to forget even when forgiving.

A parent's responsibility is a foundation for happiness in the future of their child. Togetherness with two-way respect breeds bonding. My mother did it all—but at the same time I felt the stress of trying to make ends meet. What am I saying?

WHERE IS THERE THE RIGHT ANSWER TO EVERYTHING-EMOTIONS, RELATIONSHIPS, CHILDREN, MONEY, LOVE DISCIPILINE? BETTY WOULD SAY IT IS TAKING LIFE ONE DAY AT A TIME AND LOVING ALL THE LESSIONS LEARNED."

**Your author took fifty years to recognize all this information, and still has issues putting it into practice." **

Greta told Ava; "How beautifully Katherine's house was decorated; the children are pitching in nicely." She continued, "Rita and I will fly to Clayton for a couple of days after things settle down. Rita needs to rest and get away from the situation-she was becoming very frustrated. Katherine's husband wanted to take care of his wife-and to be honest Rita was in the way."

Katherine has an unusual relationship with Rita. When she wanted to know something or needed something Rita was there-but otherwise: she likes having her mother come to dinner or talking on the telephone. It was her father she saw and talked with more often. "My mother is different-staunch in her ideas." Katherine would say "My mother is a real prude-she always wants to fix everything. She drives me crazy at times; I don't know where she gets her ideas. My father says she is a good woman. I know that to be true-but I do not need her wisdom or experience—the one that counts is my dad."

Chapter 60

Wisdom Born of Age

Landing in Rome, Ava's agent met her at the airport and drove to the apartment he rented for her and her mother. It was perfect; two bedrooms two full baths a big sitting area, a pullman type kitchen and a patio. The building was close to transportation, restaurants, and everything they would need.

The Monday of the second week in Rome Greta called Ava with the good new "Katherine did not have cancer; but as a precaution a hysterectomy was performed!" Their conversation moved on to whether Ava had been to the gallery. Have you met "Antoinette and Vincenzo?" Greta asked." Ava said, "There is a luncheon meeting set up for Tuesday." Greta assured Ava she be in Rome Friday morning since the opening was on Saturday evening.

Tuesday morning, Ava was delayed twenty minutes getting a cab. She needed to get to "Kalogeria's." for that special meeting. She picked this restaurant to confirm the raves given her by three restaurant critics. The limo driver tried his best but with heavy traffic Ava arrived there forty minutes late.

The kind hotel clerk agreed to call the restaurant for Ava and leave a message with Antoinette, apologizing for her being late. A table had been reserved for the meeting. When Ava arrived both Antoinette and Vincenzo were waiting as well as a surprise guest. During the introductions Antoinette asked to be called "Toni" and Vincenzo asked to be called "Vincent."

The introductions then moved on to a very distinguished looking gentleman with sandy brown hair and a business suit. Toni introduced him as "Grant Westfield," their attorney from Chicago. As Ava reached over to shake his hand, the man stood up to and extended his hand and *Ava thought -wow is he tall,* his big hazel-blue eyes- were as beautiful as an ocean. As their hands met Ava thought his handshake was recognizably firm.

He looked to be about 240-250 pounds with a great smile; he was the tallest person at the table. Vincent said, "Grant is 6'6" and the tallest man I ever met and the smartest attorney in the world." Toni liked him as well. She said, "Grant came to Rome for the opening of the new gallery; and to help us purchase it."

They couple met Grant a year ago when they were in Chicago buying artwork.

Ava could not help herself from noticing Grant's demeanor, soft spoken, listening attentively to the interview questions adding comments to move things along. He even engaged Ava in conversation about her assignments in Europe.

Ava glanced at this hand he was not wearing a wedding ring. Their eyes locked several times, and they shared a smile. By the end of the lunch Ava found herself interested in knowing more about him. But she also reminded herself *"she was not looking for a man or another involvement let alone a husband; and for sure she was not going to fall in love or trust him."*

When lunch was over, her cab was waiting she asked if anyone needed a ride to their hotel. Vincent and Antoinette had their car waiting. But Grant said he would appreciate a ride to his hotel. Ava agreed to drop him off.

Grant's hotel just happened to be across the street from where they turned off to her apartment. As she dropped Grant off, she gave him her card with her telephone number-just in case he had any further questions or thought of things she should add to her article.

Grant thanked her for her telephone number, the ride, and said it was a pleasure meeting her. The two shuck hands again and parted. Ava's thoughts were running wild *"He sure is a looker. I need to remind myself regularly that I am not going to care about anyone or get involved.*

As the driver took her to her building *Ava wondered why such an attractive man was not married. She resolved to not question him regarding marriage-she needed information necessary for her article and he was not part of her assignment.*

When she arrived at her apartment, she turned on the TV and prepared to take a hot bath. There was something on the news that got her attention-a riot in Chicago. She became concerned about her mother who was still in Chicago. She put through a call. Greta answered and assured her that she was fine and would be arriving on Friday as planned.

Ava mentioned Grant Westfield and to her surprise her mother commented that she and Grant have been on many such openings together before." Greta said, "Grant was a confirmed bachelor, thirty-four years old and a sharp attorney. As the story goes, he was very much in love while he was in law school. They broke up and she married someone else."

All that served to do was entice Ava more to learn about the man—as an inquisitive reporter –of course! Ava sat down and checked her messages. There were a number from her editor and one from a stranger: Mr. Elliott Alban. He left a strange message "Miss West, I would like a few minutes of your time. I was a friend of your father, Slade West. Please call me?" Ava decided to wait until her mother arrived before answering that call.

The next day Ava spent the day checking out the gallery's ads and invitation list. She wanted to get familiar with the names and have her agent check out who these people were and what they were affiliated with so she could ask intelligent questions at the opening. She asked Greta about the name Elliott Alban" but Greta never heard the name of the man, she left a message with Mr. Cantor's secretary and asked him who the man was and what he might be wanting with her.

Mr. Cantor was out of the office for two more days; Ava left a message asking him to call her.

Chapter 61

Things get Interesting

The sun was shining, and the air smelled fresh and clean as Ava met her mother at the airport. Greta looked beautiful she had on a tan jacket with a melon-colored top and a pencil skirt. She had someone with her, at first Ava was unable to see--then the lady turned around and to her surprise it was her Aunt Rita. "We thought we would surprise you dear," said Greta. I invited Rita to stay with us for a while. Everyone exchanged a greeting and hug. "This is indeed a pleasant surprise, how are you Aunt Rita?" she asked. "I am a bit nervous my dear this is the first time I have been out of the United States you know." Ava spoke. "No, Aunt Rita I did not know. I would have never guessed you are so cosmopolitan. Was this a last-minute decision? She asked. But before anyone could answer Rita said, "I was happy that Katherine did not have cancer. I wasn't needed there any longer. Then Greta offered me this trip so the three of us could spend time together. What a great opportunity how could I turn it down." "Great a lady's only trip!" Ava said.

Arriving at the apartment Ava was trying to decide the sleeping arrangements. The apartment had only two bedrooms a small kitchen and living area. Greta announced, when Rita agreed to join us, she contacted their press agent, he then rented an apartment on the third floor for them; they move tomorrow. It is a three-bedroom, three bath place with a full kitchen and living room. AP is picking up all the cost as Rita is exploring the education system in Europe to answer questions that may enhance the article you will be doing in the future.

Ava knew her mother, Greta always figured out a way to do something she wanted. For their first night Greta and her daughter sleep together. It was reminiscent of days past when Ava would run into her mother's bedroom to get warm.

The ladies talked for about two hours then wanting a light lunch at the apartment; they then went for a walk and shopped at "Louie's Italian Deli" for Scillian salami, olives, the Italian ham prosciutto, hard crusted Italian bread and of course cheese." When in Rome do as the Romans and enjoy the food which is outstanding and the architecture of course!

That night they dined in the Hotel Palazzo. To Ava's surprise Grant Westfield walked in and came right over to their table. "Hello Greta" he said and then added "Good evening, ladies." Greta greeted him with a hug and kiss. Then Grant asked, "Am I late?" "Not at all" Greta said as he took a seat at the table. Greta introduced Rita and then said, "I believe you have met my daughter Ava." "Yes, I have Greta it is easy to see she is your daughter –she has your good looks." Ava gave her mother a stare; the two women shared a moment of "mother knows best."

The discussion at the table was not about the gallery at all, but about Rita's involvement with the Chicago school board. Grant recently accepting a position as the board's legal counsel. Rita wanted to be sure he would be able to support her with the changes she had been suggesting. Since her daughter was in the hospital and Grant was in Rome the two had not been able to discuss her suggestions. Grant declared he was a terribly busy attorney traveling with 30-35% of the time away on business.

While he accepted the position with the school board it was with the reservation that members of the board agree to find another attorney within ninety days.

Greta and Rita "worked" on him to reconsider to no immediate avail. Ava just listened. The ladies were relentless and by the end of the two-hour dinner Grant reluctantly agreed to consider the position for up to a maximum of one year.

Greta picked up the check and they all left the restaurant. At the door Grant thanked the ladies for dinner. He told Greta she had brought along two equally beautiful women and he must have been trapped by their beauty as he could not seem to refuse them anything.

Greta said, "Now Grant, it was just the logical explanations of the changes needed-that really convinced you." Grant laughed and said, "Well Greta you are one of the best presenters I have met; cornering me with your Aunt Rita."

Chapter 62

A New Beginning

At the apartment Ava had questions for Rita and Greta. "What was this trip and dinner all about Mom?" Ava asked. Greta announced when she learned Grant was in Rome" and Rita added with "knowing the school board had been trying for a month to meet him, we decided to set him up and it worked." Rita thanked Greta for her help. She began putting through a call to the head of the school board to announce their success.

While Rita was on the telephone Ava began packing things for their move in the morning to the new flat. Greta was helping her.

Now mother and daughter alone they found an opportunity to discuss Grant Westfield.

Greta said, "Grant knew all about Rita's proposals he did not want to vote on them or accept the challenges they initiate. But Rita wanted his vote, and this was the best way to get his attention and commitment. It was all planned in advance Honey."

The next morning the three women went to see their new apartment on the third floor. It was not as pleasingly decorated as the apartment they were leaving. This one needed: to be painted, have new drapes and different furniture.

Greta called the building super. She would not move in until the apartment was painted, and she wanted new the drapes and furniture before they moved into this apartment. The man argued; "The new tenant would be moving in at 3 PM to Ava's place." She said, "Too bad-just cancel that person's move until this place is competed." The super protested "I do not think Mr. Westfield would like that Miss he is in a hotel and does not like where he is staying." "Mr. Westfield you say?" Greta asked. "Yes, and he wanted to be sure to move in today." The super said.

"Call him and tell him he could move in after you paint the upstairs apartment; and have it painted before 3 PM moving all the furniture and drapes from the second floor to out apartment. It is your choice" Greta said. Greta left the super mumbling, but fifteen minutes later there were three men upstairs moving furniture from Ava's original apartment to the third floor to the apartment.

The super came in "Ladies if you will move now, we guarantee these three men will paint the living room and kitchen tomorrow?" Greta agreed and the move was in process just as Grant arrived. He did not expect to see Greta in the hall. He was also amazed that it was their apartment he was going to be living in for the next month.

Ava and Rita were in the new apartment giving the men directions about the placement of the furniture when Greta and Grant arrived. "So, it is you ladies that I have to thank for that old sofa being put in my apartment and those flowered drapes."

All of them had a good laugh. Grant helped the ladies finish their move by bringing all the food from their refrigerator upstairs. "Since there are three women in this apartment may I presume you, all know how to cook-and I should be invited up at least occasionally due to all my help in bringing your refrigerator items to this floor. And do not forget my endurance of flowered drapes in apartment of a bachelor?" The ladies all agreed to invite him and promised to find more suitable drapes for his apartment.

After the move Greta went to the superintendent of the building and asked if there were any other apartments available. He showed her two others and low and behold one had beautiful blue drapes and a new furniture. She gave the super $10 American dollars to move both the drapes and the sofa into Grant's apartment in the morning when everyone was at breakfast. He agreed.

On her way back, she knocked at Grant's door and invited him to breakfast. She said nothing to Rita or Ava about what she had just done. She told them Grant was meeting them for breakfast at 8 AM. The next day everything went as planned the ladies made breakfast consisting of coffee, bacon, eggs, potatoes, French toast, and fruit. Grant enjoyed all the food and when breakfast was over Grant thanked them and proceeded to his apartment.

Opening the door to his apartment; the new blue drapes and sofa impressed him. One of the men said, "It was the lady on the third floor she made us do it. She must have what she wants." Grant immediately went back upstairs to thank them. When Greta opened the door he said, I know you well enough Greta to know you arranged to have the new drapes and furniture put into my apartment this morning. How did you arrange it? Greta answered, "It was nothing that a little negotiating could not do." When he left both Rita and Ava wanted to know how Greta arranged all the changes to be done during breakfast? Ava knew her mother could do anything but in Rome! They all had a great laugh as Greta answered, "I sort of asked and did the trick with $10 for each of the three men and the super!"

The next day the ladies spent time showing Rita the best shopping area. This did not leave time for much else. As that night was the Gallery's Grand Opening. The festivities were to begin at 8 PM.

The ladies were dressed beautifully; Rita was in a Champaign colored fitted dress, with a silk shawl around her shoulders, her hair was in French twist under a small, netted hat. Her auburn hair looked lovely, and her brownish golden colored shoes completed her purse and gloves.

Greta wore cobalt blue dress with a jacket that covered her breast and went down about two inches it buttoned down the back. She carried a cobalt and white clutch purse she had the same matching shoes and gloves. She had a large silver pin on her jacket.

Ava wore a Black dress with a low back and a bow where the back of a bra would be, white gloves and black and white shoes, purse and hat. The trio looked beautiful. Over 300 people attended the opening, and it was a great success.

Grant Westfield welcomed all three ladies and complemented them on how beautiful they looked. He left them and spent the evening with an older woman the ladies did not know. Just before leaving Grant came over with the woman—Ladies I
would like you to meet Mrs. Ariana Pelzer. She was the owner of this gallery until we gently convinced her to sell. Grant was taking her home. As he left it became clear to Ava that Grant took care of major clients and obviously Tony and Vincent wanted to buy the building and Grant made that possible.

Greta decided to show Rita a bit of Rome's night life. Ava decided to complete her story. Tomorrow Greta needed to learn about the St. Patrick's Day festivities soon to begin.

After completing her article Ava was tired and needed to talk a walk and have a bit of Italian Gelato." She left Greta and Rita a note identifying where her short walk from the apartment; would end up, identifying that the streets are well lit and filled with people so stop by."

While she was ordering her Ice Cream, Grant came in with a young lady. He greeted Ava and introduced the woman as his niece Margo who would be staying with him for a week.

Ava found herself intrigued and unusually attracted to Grant; deciding to see more of him she invited the two of them to dinner the next evening.
Grant thanked her but declined the invitation. 'Unfortunately, all our time is booked solid plus we have dinner arrangements every evening 'til Margo leaves." It did not leave too much room for negotiation. Ava said that if any of their plans changed just to let her know.

When Ava returned to the apartment her mother was there— "Dear, I planned to have dinner tomorrow evening with friends. I wonder, if you do not have any plans, could you join us?"

"Yes mother" Ava said in a drawl voice. "Who are we going to dinner with?" "Mr. Charles Strobeck" Greta answered. Mr. Strobeck is the owner of one of the Syndicated Press service companies here in Rome." Ava felt it would be a boring evening but agreed when Greta said they were going to "Mario's for a special stuffed Lamb entre."

The ladies met Mr. Strobeck at "Mario's" restaurant at 7 PM. The evening was spent discussing his opening a paper syndication in Naples with high hopes for its success. Mr. Strobeck was 64 years old, six foot tall with graying hair. He was about 200 pounds and a widower for the last seven years. He took to Rita in seconds, but she kept him at arms distance.

When the evening was over, he asked if he could call her. Rita was kind but firm. "I appreciate your offer. I am sure my husband would love to see your vineyards, but I will have to ask for a rain check. We have planned every day until I leave for Germany"

"Germany?" Ava knew nothing about Rita going to Germany. When the ladies returned to the apartment Ava asked about Germany. Rita said she was invited to a conference for three days in Germany and was leaving the day after tomorrow. The conference was about the educational differences in teaching and programs in Germany and the success they have had with grades and scores. She would be attending the conference and then leaving from Germany to return to Chicago. Her plane would leave on Monday evening.

Ava said her conference sounded like it would be excellent to add to her article. Rita suggested Ava join her. Ava agreed to think on it, but first she needed to check with her editor to have all expenses paid. Rita's leaving

Rome in one-day; both women were going to miss her. Rita suggested they visit her in Chicago.

Greta suggested to Rita instead of going home after the conference in Germany why not join them in Switzerland.
She did not need to return to work for another three weeks, they were going to Switzerland to relax and enjoy. To help Rita decide Greta asked her agent change Rita's tickets. "Press has its privileges." Since there was no cost involved Greta felt confident there would be no way Rita could object. Add that to both ladies prompting and encouraging her to join them and Rita agreed.

Rita enjoyed Europe and the idea of spending more time with Greta and Ave felt wonderful-how could she refuse. Besides, Carl was traveling to New York to be with Shana, so she really did not have to rush back to Chicago.

Meanwhile in New York, Carl was expounding on the issues of his marriage with Dr. Bryan Meyer. Bryan was an old college friend of Carl's the two men stayed connected. Dr. Meyer was a successful psychologist. He was in New York visiting one of his daughters. Byron's daughter needed help with one of her sons, Galvin. The boy was involved with the wrong crowd and his father would not get involved since the divorce. Consequently, Bryon came to help her with the boy.

The men decided to meet for lunch. Both men were frustrated.

Carl was puzzled-he was not happy in his marriage -but now with Rita thinking of moving into one side of the new multi-family house; he did not want her to move there without him. Carl wanted Rita to change he "hated her giving him opinions on his business. She talks about stuff she reads all the time, that I have no interest in; she acts like she understands my work-but then asks a million questions, she knows a little about my research, and wants to give me suggestions. Yes, we have children together and financially we are better off together. Still, I am at a loss for what to do. Should I get my own apartment like her father did." He asked.

Dr. Meyer answered him this way, "Carl do you want your own apartment?" Carl answered, "I never thought about it-Rita has always been home." Meyer stated Rita has been in Rome for three months and now she is staying for another two weeks." He continued "Did/do you miss Rita?" "Did/do you love her in the beginning/now; or was it just the desire to help her from her past? Did you marry her for the comfort she was able to provide you until you could get on your feet-or the funds you needed, or because you were madly in love with her? When you made love to her did you love doing that or was it just an act?" "Rita is a science teacher do you..."

"Stop! Stop!" said Carl loudly. "Rita is not a raving beauty, but she is attractive, a good cook, and she loves working and keeping busy. We did not fight often-but …I…but I just do not know. I know we love our children. I see Shana in New York as I pass through there going to my lectures every chance I get. Rita is always helping Katherine and Joseph Carl, or her family let alone all the grandchildren."

Bryon said, "Carl, I am at a loss for words and cannot recommend anything to you. Carl, you need to answer truthfully the questions I proposed. Possibly living in your own apartment, you will be able to sort out your true feelings and values."

When Carl spoke of traveling soon with his grand-daughter Bryon told him "That was an excuse from having to face truth and make important real decisions. You should be traveling with your wife, and you should be happy to do that and have her as part of you program. I am confident other presenters have their wives with them—am I not correct." "Yes, most of them do," said Carl."

"That is a cop out because you niece looks up to you; you could make all the decisions with a sweet little thing looking up to you. It is a runaway from bringing your wife. If you don't love her or want her then let her find another man and you find another wife." "But Byron," Carl protested, "I have never found another woman I want to be with; most of them are women who have been divorced coming with baggage and just wanting me to pay their way or give them what they want." Many have raised their children and now have grandchildren—I have my own children and grandchildren."

"Well Carl all you seem to want is your freedom to go and do or take with you whomever you want—so you do not need Rita-right?" Byron said "What—now your being ...I don't know." "No Carl—you don't know, and you should find out before it is too late." Byron said. "Understand Carl, what is your happiness and how does Rita fit in—then choose Rita or whatever—but if it is not Rita than you should tell her so she could make a life for herself."

Chapter 63

A Long Way Home

After Rita left for Germany, Ava and Greta went to the theater, enjoyed a dinner at a special restaurant and then left for visited sites in Naples. Rita called and left a message that her plans changed. She received a call from Shana; Carl was not feeling well. She decided to return to Chicago, if the truth be known, she loved Carl and wanted to take care of him. She hoped of returning one day to finish their exploration of Europe.

Greta and Ava got the message from their agent when they were in Naples. returning to Rome they did not see Grant until the end of their second month in Rome.

He was getting ready to return to Chicago and invited the ladies to dinner at Marco's. The restaurant opened a new place near airport. He suggested an early dinner since his flight took off at 7:15 PM. Ava was not able to make the dinner-she was assigned to cover a large sale took place at the Gallery. The painting sold for two million dollars and was being shipped to Germany.

Greta decided she would go to the gallery and asked Ava to meet Grant. Reluctantly Ava agreed to meet Grant. The two of them discussed their travels. Grant said he would be traveling to China in three weeks on business and would be gone for at least a month. One of Ava's dreams was to spent time in China and Hong Kong. It was a childhood dream. Grant was kind and polite but not very personable or very friendly.

As he was leaving, he said "Next time you are in Chicago-please look me up; I would love to listen to how things are going with your articles—maybe we could have dinner together." Ava said, "That is very kind of you Grant."

She watched Grant leave the restaurant and head to airport. As he left Ava thought *"I finally met a man that spurs my interest, and he is off to travel around the world. Oh, well-I am still not going to be involved with any man, so this does fit in to my plan."*

A Long Way Home
Con't

Ava and Greta stayed in Rome for the full three months it was wonderful, the loved all the delicious meals and they pampered themselves often.

But Ava was happy to be back to be on US soil and home. Suddenly, Greta accepted an assignment in Switzerland. And it was planned for the two of them to be there for fifteen days. Their hotel was beautiful hotel was right in the middle of the town in Zurich. They enjoyed great restaurants and relaxing near the pool. It was a perfect place. While in Switzerland, Mr. Storbeck called Greta. He inquired if Rita was with them. Greta explained "Rita went to her husband as soon as she learned he was not feeling well." He asked that Greta mention to her he was asking if she had joined them." Greta agreed. It was obvious that Mr. Storbeck was attracted to Rita.

This trip was the final straw for Greta. She was tired of traveling and decided she would sit out the next three months. Ava suggested visiting Rita in Chicago. This would give her an opportunity to take Grant up on his offer. But unfortunately, Rita found the timing not right. Carl had been ill, and a stress test identified Carl's heart valves was clogged, and he would need a minor surgery. Rita wanted to be there with him.

Greta accepted an invitation to visit friends in Fort Erie for dinner. Ava was bored and feeling alone only a week of being home. She found herself drawn once again to the journals. She looked through the pages for something that intrigued her.

"Michael and Nora are so much in love. They have lived through lot together and have come out on top. I do not understand how. Tonight, Michael told everyone they would be-renewing their marriage vows in three weeks. He asked if we would all join them for a celebration. That would be their 38th Wedding Anniversary. I really wonder what their secret is because they have a great marriage.

I was present when the two of them disagreed on raising Greta and fought. Somehow, they worked out parenting and loving-and to this day I am baffled."

The next entry was dated about two months later. There was a card pasted in the book. It was the invitation to Michael and Nora re-taking of their vows at St. Andrew's Church and a dinner.

"Nora was a beautiful bride for the second time. She was dressed in a simple beige knit two-piece suit with a pill box hat, beige shoes, gloves and a dark beige clutch bag. As she walked to Michael his eyes were on her and they were obviously filled with love. It was so nice watching the two of them so much in love with each other. It must have been strange having a pregnant daughter walk them both down the aisle.

Greta looked radiant, six months pregnant with Ava, and so proud of her parents. There were twenty of us at the wedding and at the dinner. The weather outdoors was perfect for the wedding, and everyone enjoyed the service. I just wish Kevin would have gotten the message."

Once again Ava felt her great grandmother—must have had a hard road being in love and getting nothing in return.

As she thumbed through the pages in the book Ava read a sentence here and there, but it was not until she got to the middle of the journal that she decided to read the entire section. It was a letter from Rita:

"Betty,

I am not alone God is with us all-always. I am trying to let go of all the headaches and the arguments even my loneliness. I choose to have peace and move forward with my life. I have released the feelings of regret about this marriage. I cannot change what has happened in the past, but I can change my future.

When I decided to stay with Carl, I made up my mind to just to let him do whatever it is he wants to do. Financially we are better off together. And for the children this will work out well. I will just do what suits me and there never will be a problem.

Emotionally – well that is where the difficulty has been, but I have made up my mind to survive. I am embowered by an ability to forgive. One needs to tread water carefully. In my case it was not long, and something happened that told me nothing between us had changed. With Carl it was his trip—he was asked to give a lecture in New York City. He was not interested in my being with him-he would be "busy most of the time." Our relationship has never been the same. Trust is what Carl needs more than anything else. I am not sure I totally trust anyone these days. Why should I? I know that Carl gives me time, he does errands, he mails packages to whomever—isn't that a form of love? Doing deeds-for another is a form of love.

You know Betty, trying to understand love is extremely hard because it means different things to different people.

I found my answer. Not only do I love the man, I married, but I made a vow in front of God. I am empowered by conscience, loyalty and love of Carl and my love for God. Carl is a good man-a good doctor and a good father when he needs to be. Life provides a learning curve. It is all a choice.

We learn how to survive the twists and turns of love, how to understand the meanings of love - and we learn things in general about people. I believe Carl when he says he is "committed' to me. We are comfortable being with each other. That and my love for him, and our children keep us together. How about you and my dad, Betty—have things changed since John married?

Love, Rita"

"I wrote Rita, and this is a copy.

Rita, everything has changed. While we are not where we were fifteen years ago--Kevin laughs more. There are times he forgets his resentment and anger. Kevin is a stubborn man, but he has been mellowing.

I guess the old saying of "Never give up" has merit. I have always tried to let him know that I love him.

He recognizes I am here, and I try to take care of him-if he lets me. He says "thank you" when he remembers. He seems locked inside from showing anything else. I cannot bring him out of that state.

He loves Michael and Rita but stays at arms distance with both. I still get the silent treatment but it of no consequence any longer. I can deal with that better these days than when it first started to happen.

Love, Betty

Chapter 64

Love from Betty

October

So many things have happened in these last three years

I just do not know where to begin. We both have so many physical issues, it was hard to keep up with the maintenance on the house, so we decided to sell the house.

We started looking into apartment together - before the actual move was to take place Kevin decided he wanted to go into senior place on his own. You could have floored me. As we were settling on where to live, he made arrangement to move into a senior residence in a small room, preparing to move he threw out 80% of his clothes and belongings. He did not want anything to do with furniture. The house was sold so I had to move he moved out before it even closed-just went to the lawyer and signed the papers. I had four days to clean out the house and move into an apartment on my own. I thank God for Michael, Nora, Greta, and Ava because I was going out of my mind.

I found an apartment only two buses from where Kevin moved. Michael had his men move me; Nora and got the house ready for the new people. I used to visit him twice a week-but he avoided me and would leave his room and go out to the group with me sitting there. He enjoys flirting with the women, even acts younger when he gets their attention. He plays cards with the men and jokes with everyone of the staff; but for me-he has nothing to say. For Christmas I brought him a new sweater and made a tray of his favorite cookies; when I walked in, he took the tray from me and passed my tray around until it was empty-never eating one or saying thank you. He looked at me like I was a stranger. I will no longer accept his rudeness or his indifference. If I get the chance and feel up to it, I may visit him again.

When I got the call from the head of the senior center that Kevin passed away in his sleep, I made all the arrangements for his burial-just like he once told me he wanted. I buried him near Mary Jo. He left me a sizable amount of money. I sold the two plots that we originally agreed to be buried on. I purchased a plot near my mother.

After our house was sold Michael and Nora sold their house; they moved into an apartment across the street from my apartment to be near me. They are so much in love I envy them.

Ava has brought a joy to the whole family. Her presence changed us all-there is peace, joy and love all shown because of that child. Greta was so right when she said Ava was a gift to us all.

Six months after I moved into my apartment, Charles approached me, he has stage four lung cancer, he smoked for years He asked me to help him, not physically because he has nurses, but with taking care of the house, cooking and laundry. He offered me rent free. He was concerned I would have to use all my money to keep up the house.

He said he would pay for everything including the food. I spoke to Michael and Nora, and they were good with it. Charles is devastated-neither his daughter nor her husband would even consider bringing his grandchildren to see him. He is so deflated. I do hope all grandchildren would learn how bad that decision was to hurt grandparents. John and his wife left Clayton. They now live in Florida.

John gave Charlie the house; they both gave Michael their interest in the construction business. Except for the alarm system John sold off the system; and will receive royalties all his life. John and Charlie sold the monitoring system the brothers divided the royalties three ways Charlie, Michael and Rita.

Kevin was not happy with how John arranged it. But the brothers knew Kevin's feeling about Carl, as he openly was upset with Rita and planned to leave her only a small amount of money as an inheritance. Michael and Charlie will get one-third each and Rita will get the other third. John said, "Rita is one nice lady, I hope this helps her." John said his money for the royalties will go to Charlie first and then to Rita when they are both gone. This man met Rita just once and has concern for her future. The royalties from this alarm system will be in the thousands. Amazing!

Katherine will have a baby soon. Her brother Joseph Carl will be getting married in a month. The family is growing. When Greta moved back to Clayton—my little love wanted to be near me. Greta purchased a house one block away.

Everyone loves Ava. When she calls me Great Grandma I melt. When I die, I will leave everything to Ava."

Chapter 65

Wisdom

Ava put the journal down. She thumbed through four more of them and there was nothing else that meant anything to her. The crux of writing was about dinners, holiday issues or gifts. There were cards and letters sent back and forth but nothing of real value except this one from Betty:

"Now it is time to write my will, I am not well and up in age. Charlie left me a lot of money and he gave me the house. The cash I have is enough to buy things to leave for Ava furniture I know she will love in the sewing room. Everything I own will go to Ava. I love her so I hope she understands just what her love has meant to me? Her life gave me what I needed-strange, but she brought me the most joy of everyone and that included Kevin. She telephoned me every day to tell me "Hello" and talk about her day. Then, every evening she called to say good night. When they moved back here, she came to see me during the day after school-and she still called me to say good night. This child brought me so much happiness-my heart rang a bell for true unconditional love. The child was a gift to us all."

Just then Ava saw an envelope sealed in the back of the book. It was addressed to Ava. With tears in her eyes, she opened the envelope.

"My Dear Ava,

I love you more that I could every express in words.

Your love has been what has sustained me all these years. You were three years old when Greta taught you to begin calling me every day. You did that until...

I leave you everything. The keys in this en-velope are keys to two safe deposit boxes. It has been paid for until you are twenty-five. It is held by the Clayton Main Bank go there and be surprised." If you haven't found these keys by then Greta will be notified that the boxes are in trust for Ava West's twenty-fifth birthday."

Love, Greta Grandma Betty"

Ava was in tears. First the house, then the furniture what else could there be? She dialed her mother and told her of the letter. Greta was just as curious as Ava. "Go and see what is there" she said. The next Monday morning Ava went to the bank. The box was number sixty-nine and seventy. Ava had both keys. The bank needed to have identification but once they were sure Ava was the intended person, they gave her the boxes. In a room Ava looked at the first box box-it was large safe deposit box-not like the second one that was much smaller. She sat down and lifted the pin to open the box. In the box was term US bonds that would come due when Ava was twenty-five. There was stock that John gave her from the company that bought his alarm system. Today that company is a major "player" in alarms. Finally, there was pictures of Betty, Kevin, Great, and Ava.

In the second box was all of Betty's jewelry, her wedding rings, diamond earrings, necklaces and Kevin's wedding ring. There was also a small gift box with a knot tied on the top it was marked for "Ava on her birthday" in the box were 16 pieces of wrapped items. Ava opened each one carefully. Betty had bought a piece of solid gold bullion as birthday gifts each year for Ava. There was sixteen pieces of solid gold, The next year for her sixteenth birthday she bought diamond earrings for Ava. Then for her twenty-first birthday she bought a diamond necklace to match her earrings. She died just before Ava reached her 18th birthday.

As Ava opened the wrapped pieces she gasped. Oh my God. She left everything in the safe deposit box. When she arrived home, she called Greta. Greta was just as shocked as Ava. The ladies felt that Betty was a true gift to all the family-not only was she honest but also loving of everyone. Ava decided to just leave the items in the box. She did not need them at this time, and they would be security for her future. She told Greta that "It was a great feeling knowing that your birth put life into a family that had been through so much pain and for so long."

Ava felt that her birth must have been part of God's plan to help this family. She was not a mistake, but a choice God made for them all. Betty placed a small notebook of only fifteen pages in the box. Ava took the book put it in her purse and decided to read it that night before bed. On the notebook were the words "Pearls of Wisdom."

Chapter 66

Family

Arriving home, Ava decided not to check the notebook until later. She did the laundry, made supper and sat down to read the paper. She looked at the words written on the notebook from Betty. She had placed the book on the end table near the sofa where she was sitting reading the newspaper. The words "Pearls of Wisdom" caught her eye. She decided to read a few words.

The first was:

"Love God with your whole heart, mind and soul."

It was followed by the following:

"God's love is given freely to us not because of what we do –but because of how we love him, follow his rules."

"Know who you are-study your ways and make up your mind to be the person you were meant to be. He made you for a reason."

"St. Paul wrote that everyone wants to be accepted, loved, and cared for –therefor have peace in knowing that God is always there for you."

"Live" your days with a sense of confidence and courage."

"Life will always have sorrow and pain, use wisdom, understanding, and peace to get through the challenges."

This one was difficult for me: "Love unconditionally, accept people even though they are NOT how you want them to be."

"Everything in life is a choice; therefore, learn to make good ones."

"Appreciate everything in your path-they are lessons to guide your choices."

"There is a virtue in attitude. Our thoughts control us –chose to think good thoughts."

I love you Ava big time always. What I wouldn't give to hug you now.

Great-grandma Betty

Ava loved the little book. She thought: *It was like reading a book on psychology or philosophy I think it would be good to read a page every night. I absolutely loved how Betty smiled at me. She always had time to read to me, we did so many crafts together, and sewed doll clothes together. Betty came to all my school plays she was always a part of our holiday. We made the best cookies together and we both loved to shop. Great-grandma Betty was the best girlfriend a child could ask for; we talked about everything—and she knew how to keep my secrets-like the one where I wanted a black bra, and my mom said I was too young. Great-grandma Betty bought it, and mom never said a word. Or the one where I wanted to have a pair of high heel shoes---great grandma Betty took me to the store, and I high heel shoes-only they were called "Cubin heels."*

Chapter 67

Moving

The next two years went by quickly. Both Ava and her mother traveled and enjoyed writing. But all the travel was wearing on Greta in three months she would be sixty years old. Ava would be twenty-nine years old this year.

Of all the men mother and daughter met none were they were interested in beyond business. The two of them decided to return to Clayton. Ava still renting out Grandma Betty's house. She returned to live with her mother, they lived together and worked together. The people Ava rented her house to a doctor, his mother and sister all super people.

The mother loved to garden, she put in lilac bushes, roses bushes and tulips in the front and side of the house. The exterior was stunning. She even put-up little white fences that her son made working in the garage to give a professional look to her gardens. The doctor was a crafts-man with wood putting shutters on the house, and other handmade additions. Ava paid for all materials, but they all did the work. The doctor put up crown molding at the top of all the exterior windows and a window box at the lower part for flowers. All his work was artistically done and really enhanced the value and beauty of the house.

The sister was a wiz at color and paint. She re-painted the kitchen, the entrance hall, living room and bathrooms. She used a soft color and then blended it with hand crafted borders, made from wood like in the living room where she used a wane coating on all the walls. She was highly creative in the kitchen she put a beautiful ceramic border around all the cabinets. The white ceramic went from below each cabinet right to the countertop—all so beautiful. In the bathrooms she added a shower corner shelf also made from ceramic.

Because this family was so kind and kept the house in such beautiful condition along with adding value to the resale Ava gave them four month's rent free every year. She approved and paid for all supplies each step of the way, but they supplied the plans and labor. It was hard to see them leave but when she said she was selling they offered to purchase the house if Ava would hold the mortgage-she agreed.

Nora and Michael always missed Greta and Ava when they traveled. Now this last few months Greta was there all the time-. looking after her parents. She took them to their doctor appointments, managed their bank accounts, picked up their groceries. It was difficult to see them do so well in the summer but the winters –well the cold created a hardship for them.

Ava kept wondering and thinking about life. Age seems so difficult-one goes from exuberance and mobility to minimal ability, especially in the winters. Wintry weather really ages us. It creates stress. What we need it to make the most out of every opportunity when we can and find things to do indoors.

As this statement kept coming into Ava's mind, she saw her grandparents on a regular basis and had difficulty accepting the limitations of weather and their aging. She bought theater tickets and took them shopping or to the park. She thought about Greta and the fact that she was also aging. She saw her mother stressing herself out to care for her parents in the winter recognizing will need her most during that time. Greta had stopped writing. She was physically tired all the time. She and Ava did not go away at all anymore they stayed in and read or watched the television. It was a different winter, and they were looking forward to the spring and summer.

In the fall and summer Michael and Nora go out for walks, sit outside and played chess in the yard; they feel comfortable with the weather again. When Nora had a heart attack everything changed. Ava realizing there would be a time when it would just be she and her mother; and when her mother would pass away–Ava would be a—an –she could barely say the word she would be an--orphan! The thought was terrifying, and then Ava understood everything her mother was doing for her parents. It was like a light bulb of reality.

Ava thought:

We need to plan for those days and try to extend life. What about moving to a warmer climate or living in a palace?

Chapter 68

A World Opens Up

Nora pulled through her mild heart attack; she was in exceptionally good shape for her age. Michael would have been so lost without her.

When summer began Ava and Greta decided it would be nice to take her parents on a trip to Chicago. They had not seen Rita and the rest of the family in three years. This would be their last trip until next year. Too bad Michael and Nora can't travel in the winter. It would be good for everyone to live in a hot climate we all love getting together with family.

Greta made all the reservations. Rita and Carl were elated. Before the trip, Michael needed to have new shoes and they had to be "Peabody's" shoes. Well, there was only one place to get these shoes and that was in the city, so Greta took Nora and Michael out for the shoes and a special lunch.

It was at lunch when Nora said she missed all the family get togethers; too bad they all live so far away from each other..."

When Greta returned home, she prepared dinner. Ava came in and had dinner. As the two women sat at the kitchen Greta told Ava about what Nora had mentioned. She began slowly Ava… Nora said "It was too bad everyone lives so far away from each other. Being together as a family gives one life." "Please think about that statement for a minute honey.

Think about what is most important in life and how to make it happen." There was no longer anything special for them in Clayton except Nora and Michael. Oh, they had friends-but with all their travels they barely saw anyone. Nora and Michael moved back into an apartment after Betty passed away. They only had Ava and Greta… it did not take the women long to come to the same conclusion. It would take work and time, but it would give everyone family again.

That night they called Rita. Greta said, "What would you think of all of us moving to Chicago?" Shocked Rita said, "What do you mean-all? Are you thinking of moving your parents along with you and Ava to Chicago?" "Yes!" said Greta.

"I think it may be difficult for your parents to adjust to an apartment or retirement complex here-- they are older, and change is not easy. But I have an idea-may I call you back in a minute?" Rita said.

Twenty minutes later the telephone rang. "We have an idea" Rita said. "I spoke to Katherine –she and her brother Joseph Carl are talking about buying 14 acres of land. Both families were going to build on the land so their children would be closer to each other. Carl and I were also thinking of building on the adjacent land. But there is a house with an acre about 600 feet away adjacent to their land. Why don't you either build on part of their land or find land near where there is a well? If you did you could build a place for your parents, and we would all be together –without the need of a retirement home. Of course, the Chicago winters are like those in Clayton and that would be a consideration."

The idea once explored was getting a bit complicated. Greta did not think about living in a compound near all the family; nor did she consider living with her parents that close and having to take care of them 24/7. While she was tired of travel- and writing- it was just for "now" taking care of two ill parents required much more tiring commitment. She remembered how tired Nora and Michael were in caring for Lilly. She told Rita she would discuss it with Ava first and then with her parents.

Greta felt she would think about it. Rita suggested that "just in case" she would keep an eye out for any property near the intended compound." Two days later Carl phoned Greta. "I have a solution and you are going to love it. It has been difficult for Rita to want to leave the grandchildren. Our kids want to buy the land so they could have a community pool and riding stables for all the grandchildren.

When Mary Jane was in her first year of college Katherine had twins: Warren and Andrea. It was a shock, but Rita had her twins when she was that age-it must run in the family. Anyway,
Rita and I did not want to be in the middle of the children's area so we are looking at a house on the corner-so we could be always available to help.

Well, three blocks away is a new retirement home called "Our Age Enhancements." It is a retirement home like you have never seen before-and not cheap but what a place: An indoor pool, an indoor gym, and theater. And finally, there is a gallery, in which art, painting, crafts and writing is developed. Most people live longer when they are involved. There are private sitting rooms next to a bedroom. Each living area has a full-size bedroom, an "L" shaped kitchen with a small refrigerator, small range, and a full bath. There is a small pull-out table and a TV in each unit. In the summer, the residents plant a huge garden. (With a little professional help) They even can all the food not immediately used in the kitchen. The place offers full meals and an ice cream shop for residents and guests. A commissary is available for small needs. The residents like the gardening, a beauty and barber shop, a sport arena, and a game room with a pool table and card tables. A staff is available 24/7 and there are five nurse's stations for the buildings. The buildings have a tolt room for 175 guests. There is a medical center with doctors and nurses on staff 24/7 with emergency medical equipment. A double room in the new wing is available now if you are interested. The cost for the double is on the brochure which I just sent you and there are pictures. It is all in the mail. Let me know what you think—I have the unit on hold with the right of first refusal."

Greta was shocked. Carl really did check this out and it seemed like he genuinely wanted to help. The brochure arrived and the place looked fantastic. The amount seemed a bit high but still reasonable. Ava reviewed the brochure and felt that it could solve one issue "but Mom there are many more issues to consider before a move could take place like: selling your home, physically moving your parents; having them buy into the idea of living in Chicago, making sure they-we have enough funds for their life-time; them getting used to a new doctor and dentists to care for them; and then trying to decide whether we-you and I should continue to live together. What? Said Greta That last statement hit Greta hard "What do you mean you and I continue to live together?" Ava answered, "This may be an opportunity for each of us to have our own home-how would you feel about that MOM?" Greta thought about it quickly-and said, "Well my first blush is that I will miss you very much-and as I am getting up in age-being alone is going to be lonely." Ava saw the look on her mother's face and decided not to pursue this line of conversation. "What do you say we all take a trip to Chicago and explore the idea?" Greta agreed

The next morning, she began discussing the trip and the possible move with her parents. Michael and Nora agreed to do it if they were all together. It took ten days before they were on a flight. Carl picked them up from the airport. He drove them to his house in Oak Brook where Rita was waiting for them with lunch ready. They were all shocked at how well both Michael and Nora took the plane ride. They loved it. They loved seeing Rita and the fact that they were in the same house that Nora and Michael had been on visits before they felt comfortable.

Michael was amazed how short the trip was in an airplane-one hour and fifteen minutes. Every other visit the two of them made together they drove. The plane ride was quick, comfortable and the stewardesses were very friendly.

Chapter 69

God Works in Strange Ways

Michael and Nora rested a bit and enjoyed a visit from Katherine. Jeff was home taking care of their arrangements and watching the twins who were now seven years

old. Katherine spoke about family and the value of all being together. She mentioned how their children had only
seen her husband's family a few times since they moved
to Florida. Her big children were just finishing school- her
son was now in his senior year and planned to go away to
college. Mary Jane went back to school for her master's
degree. She would be finished in another year. The twins
would be in the third grade next September. Mary Jane is
engaged a man named Robert Johnson; his family moved
from Texas eight years ago to Chicago. He talks about
returning to Texas, but he is an attorney and has a job
now in Chicago. The wedding is planned for later January.

Katherine said they were going to meet Robert's
parents in two days; they are all having dinner at "Christo's
Fine Italian Dining." It is a new restaurant that just opened
in downtown Chicago. Carl will be joining us leaving
from work; Rita agreed to pick the Johnson's up at the
Palmer hotel. I would like for you and Ava to join us.
Greta and Ava agreed.

Once at the restaurant they all enjoyed the Italian
food. Mr. and Mrs. Johnson met Mary Jane in the past.
Mildred, Mrs. Johnson enjoyed meeting Mary Jane's family. The Johnsons were leaving Chicago in two days for a
month returning to Texas for a visit with family and friends.

As everyone was preparing to leave the restaurant a voice from behind Ava said "While if it isn't Ava

West and her lovely mother Greta. What are you doing in Chicago and why was I not called?" The man with the voice was Grant Westfield and Ava thought he looked even more handsome now than the last time she saw him. "Where are you staying?" he asked.

Greta introduced him to everyone only to learn than Mr. Johnson and Grant were old friends. The Johnsons had a plane to catch; in two days and they wanted to return to their hotel. Mary Jane and Robert were driving them to the hotel and the left the dinner.

Ava and Greta drove to the restaurant with Rita and Carl, Greta told Grant they were exploring the opportunity of the family moving to Illinois. Ava was shocked at his reply. "I would just love the idea of seeing more of your lovely daughter Greta" he said adding "and you, of course, Greta."

Greta gave Grant Rita's address and telephone number and mentioned that they would be looking at property the next couple of days. Grant turned to Ava and asked, "Greta would you mind if I took your daughter out to dinner tomorrow evening-that is if she would not be too tired from house shopping?" Greta answered, "I am sure she would enjoy an evening with you Grant as long as you did not keep her out too late?" Everyone laughed-here he was asking Greta about taking out Ava-at their age it was comical.

Grant went over to where Ava was sitting and kneeled next to her chair "Mademoiselle would you do me the honor and pleasure of your company tomorrow evening for dinner?" Now everyone was really laughing "I would love to kind sir-but you must remember the rule—I must not be home too late! I must get my beauty sleep." Now everyone was in stitches. Greta pulled up a chair from the adjoining table and asked Grant to sit down. He ordered a cup of coffee and began asking questions about what this special dinner was about? Rita explained that this was a first meeting with the Johnson's since the kids became engaged. Everyone had coffee and a snack, but it was getting late. Katherine and Jeff made their excuses about a babysitter and left the restaurant. Rita and Carl remained with Greta, Ava and Grant as Greta told Grant their plans to look at the retirement home for her parents in the morning.

Come to find out Grant is the Attorney for the "Our Age Enhancement" homes along with owning and interest in them. There were three homes now and looking for more land to buy and expand. He was with the director just before he stopped for dinner. He was too hungry to drive back to Chicago and saw the sign and just stopped in for a bit to eat. Greta called it "Fate that we should all meet again." Grant offered to show them around the retirement home in the morning.

Ava felt that the attraction between her and Grant was genuine even though she did not see much of him in

Italy. The next half hour they all laughed and kidded each other. Grant had a late appointment and said he would see them in the morning.

All the way home Greta, teased Ava "Such a nice Man "Not too young though." Greta said. "He is in his late forty's attractive and tall." Ava said, "He is a confirmed playboy at this age?" Greta replied. "He better not think he could play with my daughter." Ava just laughed.

The next morning Grant was there at 10 AM to take them to the retirement residence. He came in a limo with a driver and all. Grant said that having the limo allowed them to be together and talk. Ava, Greta, Nora and Michael we are going in Grant's limo when Carl decided to join them. In the car Carl asked Grant questions about the retirement home. Grant knew everything there was about the place-along with being the attorney for the group and part owner of the project. They spent three hours touring the place and even enjoyed a complimentary lunch. Grant mentioned that food was especially important to all residents but especially nice for the potential residents to enjoy. He mentioned, visitors eat off the regular menu which gives residents three choices for each meal. The food was perfect not too spicy, well-cooked and good quality mostly organic.

Nora loved the craft room and the opportunity to cook in their own apartment. Michael enjoyed the woodworking room and the fact that gardens were planted by the residents with the food being used in the kitchen. They saw that residents had both a flower and a vegetable garden going. All of them loved seeing and enjoying samples from the ice cream shop. The first-floor commissary offering some food, clothes and necessities to help make living there easier in the winter. The store had dental supplies, nail files, lipstick, toiletries, creams and a few books along with writing supplies. A bus was available to take the residents shopping every week and a small van-seating twelve to take them to appointments at no extra cost.

Grant said, "We are always open to suggestions." He then directed them to second floor and as he did, he opened the door to one of the apartments. "This apartment just became due this morning." It was beautiful – the windows faced the sun in the morning and over-looked the entrance of the building near the sitting and planting areas. The parking for the building was off to the side so it did not obstruct the view. There were four double windows that opened with screens on all the windows. The apartment had a thermostat to regulate the heat and air- conditioning a beautifully big bathroom with bars on the tub and the shower having an emergency cord, the tub was the kind that one walks in to enter. There were three emergency cords notifying the front desk and the nurse's stations of problems. Once pulled, a nurse from the closest station would enter the apartment to be sure everyone was all right. In the kitchen there was a small stove with four burners and a small oven. Next to the oven and range is a twelve cubic foot refrigerator. Nora fell in love with the apartment-it was one of the largest units available having a small dining area in front of the sitting room.

Michael spoke up "Grant we are not millionaires this place must cost a fortune?" Grant answered: "This is one of the largest places in the building. I am confident you would be comfortable here. It may be considered expensive, but have I mentioned we have agreed to offer this unit at a discount of 25%." Michael asked, "Why would you do that for us?" Grant smiled and answered "Why—so I could see Ava often-why else?"

Carl was the first one to speak up "That sounds like a terrific deal but for how long would the discount apply?" he asked. "Would as long as they are with us be a sufficient answer to that question?" Grant replied. Greta was shocked "May we think this over Grant? Moving is not an easy thing especially at their age there is much to be considered."

"I agree Greta-that is why we try to make thing easier. Once a week, three of the hospital Doctors visit the residence and see patients. There are two nurses and a house doctor always available for residents 24/7. The nurses and aids spend the entire day seeing and helping the residents. Two Dentists and two Podiatrists come once a month, but appointments must be made. In two weeks, there will be a second beauty shop on the first floor with three operators. Oh, and the Chapel will be completed in a month-right now we are just using the cafeteria. Let me show you the west wing-it is not open yet but..." They all followed Grant to a beautiful hall. "This will be music hall with all kinds of instruments available-and a band has been booked once every two weeks for dancing. The movie theater is just around the corner. And a popcorn popper will be available for the residents to have popcorn every evening."

The large fish tanks will be installed in the two entrance ways. Along with these amenities the group will have an opportunity to swim in about less than two weeks when the pools for this building are expected to be completed; the spas for this building will be completed in a month-the saunas will take a bit longer-as will the reflexology massages and other massages. We are still hiring.

The idea is to prevent exposure to the Chicago winters for as long as possible. Our staff will even have an ordering center where residents could leave a list of the groceries they would like to purchase; the staff will order, and our vans will pick up. The van charge for the residents to pick up groceries is only $1.00 each time they order plus the cost of their items.

Nora spoke up next and, in her excitement, she said "We will take it! Where do I sign?" Grant laughed and preceded to hand Greta an envelope with all the papers to register her parents. He said if they had any questions, he would try to answer them when he picked Ava up that evening for dinner. He turned to Ava and said "Would 7 pm be, fine with you?" she nodded yes. Grant walked them to the limo waiting and with that they were on their way home. Grant did not join them driving back to the house, his car was waiting at the retirement home. He mentioned to Dennis the driver of the limo "These people are precious cargo please get them home safely." He assured him he would.

All the way back to Rita's house the group talked about how the place was more a vacation place than a so-called retirement home. The residents would not even have to go out in the cold during the winter. Michael said it gave people a reason to get up in the morning with all the activities. He mentioned that selling the construction company gave then a little money to add to their retirement; but John's deal with the people who bought the security for residuals lasting 99 years and they get a third. So, the monthly cost here does not hit the budget too bad due to the discount. It appeared to Carl, Greta, and Ava that Michael and Nora were on board with the move. Next was the job of selling off Greta's house in Clayton and having items moved to Chicago from the house and Michael's apartment.

At 7 PM Grant was at their door with flowers for Greta, Nora and Rita. He gave Ava one long stem red rose.

When the two of them left Grant said they were going to another of his client's place for dinner. He assured everyone she would be home early.

He took Ava to a restaurant called "Avalon's" in downtown Chicago. The place was just beautiful. When they entered Ava saw there were private booths at the left with beautiful cherry wood settings. The restaurant was huge it seated 350. The motif was old world tastefully done with gold tablecloths and white napkins.

Grant said he had a reservation in the garden room. The room was all in glass and filled with greenery just breathtaking. The server called him by name and asked if he wanted her to begin-he said yes. Ava asked what that meant-but Grant just smiled.

The server brought in a crock of Lentil soup and Crusted Rosemary bread. Ava was shocked-and said, "But we did not order." Grant replied, "Oh but I did order, and I ordered all your favorite foods." "But how?" she asked. He laughed and said, "Thank you Greta for all your help." "My you went to a lot of trouble" Ava said. "Of course," Grant replied. Caesar Salad was next then an intermezzo and finally Lamb chops deliciously cooked in rosemary and mint with baked potatoes and asparagus. The dessert was blueberry pie and vanilla ice cream.

The dinner was delightful and the two never stopped talking. When they left the restaurant Grant drove to a quiet place with a piano bar. They danced and talked until 2 AM. Ava loved to be in his arms it was a feeling she had never experienced before. If that was not bad enough, she never wanted to leave him. When Grant dropped her off, he said he would call her. There was an awkward moment at the door Ava extended her hand to say goodbye, but Grant leaned over and kissed her ever so gently. Greta was up reading when Ava walked in. The two women spoke about her dinner and then Greta said, "I think Grandma is ready to move how about you—do you still want your own place?" Ava hesitated and as she did Greta blurted out "Carl found the perfect solution this evening. Tomorrow, we have an appointment at 11 AM so we had better get some sleep. OK?"

Ava wanted to think about Grant and how handsome he was-how polished-how he was able to take the trouble to learn all her favorite foods—she could not stop thinking about him. She must have fallen asleep. She awoke when her light went on.

Chapter 70

Chicago Here We Come

Carl moved them all along in the morning by fixing breakfast and getting them all up by 8 AM. Both he and Rita were excited. They would divide them using both cars to a secret location. Michael and Nora were not crazy about being alone all morning, but they were relaxing and thinking about the move.

Carl told them we are going to see a beautiful house. When they drove up Greta said, "It looks like a horseshoe only broad at the middle. It was strange." Carl said it was not a single family but a complex of three houses. It was built by a retired army Sargent who was left with twin daughters - that did not want to be separated when they married. The irony of the story was that the girls married twin brothers. They all wanted to live together. So, they built this home. Each section had a common wall-but the walls were soundproof and fireproof. In the rear of the property, they each had a two-car garage and a private terrace. The property came on the market two days ago and they were the first showing. Carl said it answered all our needs because it was only one mile from their children and grandchildren and the retirement home.

The first unit they entered was the smallest one it had six built in bookcases, one large bedroom, one full bath and one-half bath, the master bedroom had an alcove that was perfect for an office. The kitchen had brushed oak cabinets and a dining area open to a huge family room with a small front sitting porch--only 1075 square feet. Greta fell in love-it was private and cozy yet available.

Next, they all followed over to the unit on the far side. This 1480 square feet unit had two bedrooms, two full baths, the kitchen was decorated, and all the cabinets were white. There was-a formal dining room and a living room. However, the sitting porch was to the front and corner to the building. It seemed strange for just a moment. But they soon realized that each unit even had privacy for when they sat outside.

Then it was time to see the middle unit. It was quite large 1750 square feet. The kitchen was breathtaking with Cherry cabinets, sky lights and a huge cooking work area. There were three bedrooms two full baths and one-half baths. The place was loaded with storage areas and closets. The living room had all glass windows for viewing the yard it was also open to the dining area. There was a small room off to the right of the front entrance and just off the living room. They called that room the TV room although why no one could understand why it was an enormous size for a private office. The porch sitting was to the back of the living room facing the yard.

The entire building looked hospital clean. The front of each unit opened to a large center garden. Carl traveled much of the time, and he visited many people, but he said he never saw anything like this before. He felt it was a solution to having family and still having privacy and now cost was a factor.

The Real Estate Agent said "The best part about this complex is that –it is all separate. Each has their own utilities, taxes, entrance, garages, and expenses. The only thing jointly paid was the yard and snow removal. In the past, since it was all owned by one family, they each put up money for exterior maintenance according to their square footage." He went ahead to give each of them a copy of the listing that showed the cost of each unit. It was a no brainer-but still there were questions needing to be answered.

None of the units had any air conditioning, Rita did not like the exterior of the units, the siding on the house was wood and that could need a great deal of maintenance-painting every five years. She asked about the cost of vinyl siding, air conditioning, and the age of the roof. Greta wanted to know the heat and water bills. The agent said the property was nineteen years old. He promised to call them later with the information and answers to their questions.

When they were all back at Rita's they began discussing the options-it was agreed that siding, aid-conditioning and the age of the roof were factors that needed consideration in the cost of the property. There was the issue of hiring someone to manage the exterior- lawn and snow removal and the gardens. Carl was under the impression he had found this for Greta and Ava. With the opportunity of income but it did not take long for him to realize that Rita loved one of the units. They had been looking at a single house but in minutes of listening to the ladies Carl realized that the single house was no longer going to be a possibility.

The agent called with estimates and other information. All units needed new furnaces if air condition was going to be added. The water tank currently for each unit was 30 gallons. Rita felt they were too old and small. The old roof was only nine years old when a storm had blown away half of the pieces and a tree in the yard fell on it during the storm. The new roof put on two years ago had a twenty-five-year guarantee. The agent was able to supply the name and telephone number of a contractor who gave him them the estimate for vinyl siding. He added that all parties were now deceased and only a grand son was left that owned the entire property. He lived in Florida and was anxious to sell. The furniture in the units was available and if not wanted would be sold at auction. He also gave them the name of the attorney for the property Grant Westfield. The agent said he would be the attorney to take care of that part of the sale as well.

Greta and Rita were "gun ho" at submitting an offer and getting the furnaces, water tanks and air conditioning done as soon as possible. The siding could wait until next summer. Both Carl and Ava were not saying too much during the conversation. Carl was panting about Rita living next to her nieces-women and their stuff-he would be the only man and he feared he would be asked to take care of everything. Not something he liked-but on the other hand he traveled, and this place was not close to the airport-he could get an apartment since he was traveling a large part of the time these days.

Ava was still quite young and something inside wanted to get loose. She did not want to live with her aunt, and it was time to leave her mother. She wanted to be near the action in downtown Chicago. All night she agonized "How to tell them she wanted more—more excitement-to be around more young people. She was not ready to "hold up" in a family complex. It just did not feel right." It took her forever to fall asleep.

Chapter 71

Lessons in Love

It was almost 2 o'clock in the afternoon when Ava finally dragged herself out of bed and into the kitchen. Katherine and Rita were both crying Joseph and Carl were in the living room.

Mary Jane told Katherine that she did not want to marry Robert she wanted to live with him. She said it was "the way of the future. Marriage was not necessary until they were ready to have children." This was a shock for Katherine and everyone there.

Greta was on the telephone. Michael and Nora were sitting on the back porch. Ava grabbed a cup of coffee and went to the porch "What is going on Grandpa?" she asked. "It is all blowing up in their faces" he said. "What is?" she asked, "The idea of buying the land they were all going to live on it with their families." He said.

"Why is it blowing up and what is happening?" Ava asked. "Because first Mary Jane wants to live with her boyfriend and not get married for a year, then…" "Then what" Ava asked "then Joseph's wife—wants a divorce! She is in love with a doctor she works with—and she does not even want the children to live with her. She and her doctor want to leave Chicago—the doctor has been her lover for almost sixteen months and Joseph did not even suspect!" he said. "I cannot believe this is happening to our family first Greta, then you and now Joseph Carl." He spoke in a disgusted manner.

Ava asked, "What do you mean first Mom, then me- and now Joseph Carl?" "Your mother raised you without a father, then you got a Divorce and now Joseph will have a divorce!! And Mary Jane wants to live with a man before she marries. How can this all happen to one family? What is happening to all of you? God does not like divorce—or living with a man without marriage-we are all part of Our Lord—how can anyone think of these things." Michael continued ranting about the issues in the family, but Ava was in tears and could hold her voice no longer.

"Grandpa! Grandpa! Life is not perfect, and neither are people. God made us all different with diverse needs. Sometimes we do not understand the whys of change—l still does not understand how my father died or why Kurt was so enthralled with show business-but if Joseph's wife has another man—she has made that decision-and there is nothing anyone of us is going to do. Shit happens! And if Mary Jane and Robert want to live together-that is their choice."

Those last words did it—Michael got up from the chair and walked into the house. On his way he looked sternly at Ava- and said "You do not have to tell me Shit happens I saw it in Germany during the war—but I thought here-things would be different. I knew how things happen when one person tries to control-but marriage creates a partnership there should be a commitment, a responsibility, and a vow to each other and to God to try, to continuously work at it, to struggle through the tough times and become one. Young people want the dreams without the realities; the romance without the commitment; the TV excitement of love without the responsibilities; and to top it off you want each other to remain looking like you did when you first got married. Absolute stupidity-that is the real shit!" and with that he went into the house.

Ava never heard her grandfather talk like that before and as he was speaking, he got the attention of the rest of the family. He went into his bedroom and closed the door Nora followed him.

Joseph said that his wife had already packed her things and left before he got up. Her father was watching

Joseph's children so he could be at Rita's. His wife's parents can't believe what she has done. She wants their house listed for sale. She left and went to live with her lover. Her lover is divorced and has three children from his second wife and two from his first wife.

Joseph now has three children to raise, and he must sell the house with no place to go. Without Joseph's participation in the purchase of the 14 acres of land—Katherine's family could not complete the purchase. They had their house on the market for sale and need to stop showing that home. They will stay where they are for now.

Katherine's daughter Mary Jane interrupted the conversations and announced she was packed, leaving and moving in with Robert at his apartment in downtown Chicago. Everyone now was in an uproar.

Ava thought of a solution—she mentioned the place they had looked at just yesterday to Joseph. He called the broker and decided to see it that afternoon. If Greta and Rita bought the other two unites, he would have both available to help with the children who were 12, 10 and 6 years old. Based on the sale of his house he could easily afford the place. His wife said she wanted nothing-her doctor made enough money she will not ask for alimony. She also will not pay anything to help support their children. All she wanted was to be free.

The ladies felt that Joseph could save them the labor cost since his soon to be x-brother-in-law would help him put in the furnaces and air conditioners. His brother-in-law had the same thing happen to him three years earlier thank God they did not have any children. He was married only a brief time.

After seeing the middle unit Joseph was ready. All three of the units were vacant and that made it easy. Joseph wanted the furniture to be added to their bid in his unit-he would only take a few pieces from his home. His children had their beds and toys that would be important to them. He still needed to tell them that their mother left. Joseph's wife told them she was going away for a seminar. The kids do not know that their mother was not returning. When she left, she only had her jewelry and clothes and wanted nothing else. She and her doctor had jobs at a new clinic; that opened in Canada. She wanted an immediate divorce to be free to marry. She would call them after they were settled. Joseph was devastated-he never saw it coming. He loved her but now he had to think of his children. He was ready to sign an offer-if they were all in with the deal.

The three of them talked and agreed to give their offers that afternoon. Greta wanted to speak with Ava first she remembered her younger days and she felt her daughter desire for independence. The two talked for about an hour and finally agreed that Ava would move to the city and Greta would take the smallest unit.

Carl suggested he could get an apartment near the airport because it was time, they faced the reality of their situation. Their marriage was virtually over. Rita agreed and said she could take the other end unit.

Carl was taken back at Rita's acknowledgement of his wanting an apartment; he offered her any cash she wanted or would ever need. Just then he heard himself and what Sr. Byron told him to come to a reality with. He came to the realization that he did not really want Rita to leave him he did not want it to be over.

Rita said, "She did not care if he wanted his own apartment." There was no argument or tears. The reality was setting in what was a loving and beautiful relationship-appeared gone for good. Carl found it hard to believe Rita felt nothing and would let him live where he wanted. Rita, on the other hand, felt that he had been so indifferent, rude, and uncaring to her for all those years, letting her believe that he did not love her, forcing her to do so much alone, she might as well just give up living with someone who would not love her the way she wanted to be loved. Despite still loving Carl-she told him "It was his decision."

They each made an offer on the property section that they wanted. All made stipulations that credit be given for the old furnaces and hot water tanks. Each requested the furniture be included with the sale. They knew the cost for air-conditioning and siding would have to split according to the square feet for each unit. The broker brought the contract to Grant. When he saw the names, Grant called the executor and together they agreed to accept the offering prices and include all the furniture with the sale in each unit. The owner of the building was a friend of his and really did not need the money. Grant did not want to hold any auction to get rid of the furniture. The contract was completed that day as the executor faxed his acknowledgement and acceptance.

Grant called Greta at Rita's and asked to come over after the fax came in. He told them the furniture being included in the sale gave them an opportunity to pick what they wanted and sell the rest to pay for the repairs they wanted and needed. He also said he arranged for Nora and Michael to move into the retirement home on the first of the month as a free trial for two months. That was in four days!

Grant said the trial time would be on him-free of charge so they could check it out to see if they would be contented living there. It would give Greta and Ava a chance to return to Clayton and collect Michael and Nora's personal belonging and arrange for her house to be listed for sale while arranging a moving company move things to Chicago.

It was all happening so fast, and Grant was moving it along. Greta asked about Ava-she wants to live in the city, and we have not found anything for her yet-Grant laughed a strange laugh "I will take care of that as well leave it to me" he said.

Greta and Ava left the next day. When they arrived, Grant arranged for a company Ty-dee Movers-to pack and move their stuff including Michael and Nora's the next day. All they had to do was show which boxes was going where to whom. They needed to pack their personal items and the movers would do the rest. Grant arranged for a local real estate person to call Greta and together decide on the offering price for her house. Everything would be finished and ready in fifteen days.

Chapter 72

Chicago

Ava was amazed as her best news was yet to come. Ava's tenants asked Ava to hold the mortgage with 25% down. She agreed. The mortgage was for fifteen years, and they bought it at her price. She loved the idea of selling it to them because along with a stable amount coming in monthly, she still would still have an interest in Grandma Betty's house until the mortgage was paid.

Greta' discussed with the Real Estate Broker her willingness to hold the mortgage on a sale with 25% down as well for fifteen years. When she told her caretakers she was moving to Chicago. They were pleased as they wanted to move to Florida and be near their daughter and her family. Everything was happening as if planned and there was no time for second thoughts --they were moving to Chicago!

Grant found Ava a beautiful one-bedroom corner apartment on the magnificent mile at 535 N. Michigan for Ava. It was in walking distance to the Chicago Tribune and close to State Street. The unit was just redecorated. It was also just a hop skip and jump from where Grant lived and worked. When he telephoned her and assured her, he would love it. But if she didn't, he would give her a place to stay until they could find one, she would like. He was the attorney for the owner of the condominium.

Before they could stop to think everything from the house and the apartment was loaded and on its way to Chicago. Greta and Rita boarded a plane the same day back to Chicago.

Grant was the attorney for the property they were buying he allowed them to move in at once. Nora and Michael had their belongings delivered first. They loved their new place they raved about everything. Rita and Carl had come to an understanding that Carl would over-see the sale of their house; and he would try an apartment for a while.

The condominium at 535 No Michigan was on the tenth floor. The bedroom had wall to wall cream carpeting, the kitchen cabinets and appliances were all new. One of the bathroom walls had been opened to include an entrance door from the bedroom to the bathroom as well as a door to the bathroom from the hallway. There was a large closet outside the bathroom for linen as well as an entrance closet near the front door. The combination living and dining area had hard wood floors and an oriental rug embedding the center of the living room. Heat and air condition was included along with the availability for use of the pool and exercise rooms on the thirty third floor. That floor also had a gathering room for parties. A commissary was on the first floor with a dry-cleaners, the laundry was in the basement next to the mail room for packages.

Joseph's house sold for cash within two weeks. The kids loved being near Grandma and Aunt Greta. Grant had friends finish the basement of Joseph's place while everyone was getting ready. It was painted with rugs on the floor and the old TV was moved down there with a ping pong table for them. He put basketball hoop in the back of the unit. The three boys would be fine.

Ava and Grant became constant companions for the next six months until things finally began to settle down. Ava received a call from her agent-there was an opportunity to write an expose' about the new Pope. She needed to return to Rome. It was a fantastic opportunity and not something she could turn down. She agreed to leave in two weeks. She called Greta and discussed the assignment. Greta loved Rome so Ava invited her to travel with her. Once again mother and daughter were traveling together in Rome. Grant was not as excited about her leaving but he understood.

At a family dinner Greta and Ava announced their pending trip to Rome. Rita said, "Oh my, Rome-you ladies are so fortunate." As Rita completed her comment both Greta and Ava looked at each other their thoughts were the same. The ladies walked over one on each side of Rita "Join us!" Excitement raged through the three of them except for Carl and Joseph who were watching their hugs and screams. "What about us?" Joseph said, "Who will take care of the kids or Dad and me?"

Rita had not told Joseph or Katherine about Carl not moving with her. She put her eyes down but Greta spoke up "you will just have to miss us all-it is time you men learned to appreciate your women and anyway it is only for three weeks." Rita was overjoyed.

Carl was to give a lecture in a hospital just outside of Chicago the next week but instead he decided to help Joseph move and to look for an apartment not too far from the airport. It would be the first time Carl would be living alone in thirty-two years. *I am no longer going to worry about anything and anyone" he thought. "The rest of my life will be calm, and I will be free of any responsibilities, I hope. Time will tell, I will be living a dream."*

Carl found a furnished apartment and rented it for three months. Within a week he was tired of having to clean and straighten. Coming home to an empty apartment was not fun. He went out for dinner with friends the entire week, but it was not the same. He saw men in bars looking for company. Relationships were changing. Women wanted to control relationships and he was getting ill from rich food and eating out all the time. Evenings alone in the apartment were not enjoyable and watching TV alone just did not cut it. He missed his wife, his children and his grandchildren.

Shana was busy living in New York with four children and working in the restaurant with her husband. She was not able to visit often. When he went to see her and the children their routine was hard.

Rita always made soups and watched what he ate, they always went out with friends, and he missed her. This living alone was not what he thought or expected it would be, but he was determined to stay- in the apartment at least why Rita was in Europe. He decided to date a woman he met at the airport. She was divorced with two children both married. She was working and dressed nicely. All evening she spoke of her family and her divorce. He attempted to discuss his creams and she changed the subject. He was bored when it was time to say good night she wanted to know when she would see him again. He just said he would call her. But deep down he did not want to call her. Being single was a waste of time trying to find someone to communicate with and have something to talk about. Oh, the women wanted to go places, dancing, expensive restaurants, theater and even travel. They wanted him to spend money on them and just be with the famous doctor. Carl just wanted a nice meal and an evening at home---with Rita. While it may appear romantic to be on your own and date again one easily learns that what you are really looking for someone to share your time with and care about you. So, beginning all over may seem great but it is quite lonely for quite a while until you find someone who really cares about you. Then you begin again trying to become one team.

Chapter 73

Revelations

Rome was perfect and the ladies had a wonderful time. They extended their time to add two more weeks and the days just flew by. Rita was an experience. Neither Ava nor Greta ever spent so much time with her alone or expected the "lessons" they would learn from Rita not just about her life but about love, relationships and people were important and life changing.

One evening, after an early dinner and they were all tired from shopping they sat down to relax. Ava just turned in her article. It was four days before they were to leave Rome. Rita was in a good mood, but Ava thought Rita was a bit stuffy. This night things were different. As they sat in the living room of the apartment Rita was more relaxed and she dropped her guard. Being together with the Greta and Ava--Rita she just wanted to talk. She shared many things about her mother, her father, her childhood, her children and marriage to Carl.

She began "My childhood was so difficult. I never remember a time of just being a kid. That of course did not include the times when I was with Michael. He was my strength. Whenever things were too difficult for me Michael would sense my stress, he had a way to make me laugh. Then he would ask me if we could play a game to-gether. I remember little of our life as a family before my mother got ill. When she became ill everything changed. Dad spent so much time taking care of her. Michael. I felt in the way, but I needed to cook, clean and take care of the house. During her last days I felt sorry for them you see they genuinely loved each other. We really did not matter it was their love, being together, and their dealing with things together that mattered they talked things out together and each other compromised at separate times. They loved each other very much and struggled together and enjoyed their time together.

Michael and I suffered the loss of our mother and father who was devastated at our mother's death. Michael and I learned to work on everything together. We were young mom had no energy for play as mom was in bed all the time. I had to take care of the house cook, go to school, do the laundry, shop for groceries, along with caring for Michael. All I can remember is wishing—thinking—hoping—praying that "One day—one day there would be someone who would spend time with me, take care of me, protect me, appreciate me and love me--just for me being me! I wanted someone that would always have my trust to keep my secrets, someone who would always want me; that would have my back if there was a need; someone to make me feel wanted, appreciate being with me, proud to be with me; someone alone who utterly understood and wanted me for me. I though--hoped Carl was that man and when he wasn't I learned to live with me and appreciate who I was."

"There was a teacher who would give me her time and attention one on one to show me how to do certain things. It was nice doing things together. There was a brief time when Mom was well. But she was so focused on showing me how to do something we had no time for play or love. Later, I would rush to get done whatever needed to be as quickly as possible; so, I would be able to spend time –personal time with her. I wanted to feel like a special person-cared for and recognized. Do you understand? I wanted her to stay well and let me just hug her. That never happened-she was driven to make sure I could take care of my father and Michael. One day I cried—who is going to take care of me—of ME!" Both Greta and Ava nodded their heads that they understood.

Rita continued "I found myself just "serving needs." There was no one to show me love or appreciation." I ended up with a constant fear of rejection-of being and feeling invisible. I felt insecure, alone, used, unloved and abandoned all the time.
Then you add the death of someone you love and then there is no longer a family.

After Mom died. I was so lonely. Michael was drafted the fear of losing him was very real. What would happen to us if Michael was not part of us? War like death cheats families-it is a constant fear that comes over you-wondering what next? Every night I wrote Michael a letter. I needed to do that emotionally to keep my sanity.

When Michael left, he asked me to take care of Nora he said they would be getting married when he returned. He knew she would be lonely without him No one realized how lonely I would be without Michael. Nora was my first real friend she was interested in my life, my feelings and thoughts. And Lilly well it was like having her as my mother and Nora as my sister all at once. Lilly was an enormous influence on my life and in my understanding of who I was and who I could be with an education.

It was Lilly who helped me understand and deal with my tremendous fear of rejection and the loneliness. She gave me personal time and was genuine and caring always including me in whatever she and Nora planed.

Working at the shoe store I learned about the Red Cross. The training course and the teacher led me to the biggest part of my future. Mr. Phillips, our teacher, recognized something in me unexplainable. He gave me the opportunity to really become someone—it is hard to understand that feeling? It is euphoric and compelling. He gave me opportunity not only to work at the college but to go to college and get a free education." Finally, I was understanding my desires it was a feeling I never wanted it to leave. For the first time in my life, I felt happy –in--inside—do you understand? I cherished that feeling. I decided that school was for my future. I was ready to grab it and hold on for dear life."

Ava and Greta were mesmerized by Rita's words. She never shared anything like this before with them despite all her earlier openness this was something very deep inside her that needed to come out. That is some-thing everyone seems to need at one time or another.

She said "it was a relief when Dad met Betty. She had always hoped and prayed he would find another love. His love for Betty brought Rita a kind of freedom from worry about having to give up her life and take care of her father. When Kevin and Betty initially split up it brought back those fears wondering if she had the "responsibility" and the "commitment to do it all over again." Rita was on a roll-discussing her life she wanted to continue. It was as if she was just waiting for an opportunity. It was late but no one wanted her to stop. Ava had questions about the rape and what happened, but the time was not right to ask them. She decided to ask the most difficult question: "Aunt Rita, how did rape change your life?"

"Being raped almost destroyed my life. I expected to live with fear for the rest of my life. But then I met Uncle Carl. He was a doctor in the hospital where I was taken. He stayed in my room that first night. When I woke in fear his voice was so soft, gentle and caring. I trusted him at once. He knew first-hand about rape he saw the challenges his sister Carol faced due to her rape. Carl was living at home and saw not only what it did to her but what that did to their family. He was determined not to see that happen to me. He made himself the most important person in my life. He took me to see his friend who was-a counselor. He took me there and stayed for the appointment in the waiting room while I talked to the counselor. Our friendship began to grow we would go out for coffee, take long walks and then we would go to dinner. Carl became interested in me more than anyone in my whole life. I felt safe with him and could not think of life without him. I fell in love and all I wanted was to be with him. With him as my husband I opened to the world. The man that raped me later killed himself. He was mentally ill for years. Carl made sure I would not be mentally ill-his love gave me everything I needed to understand, cope and go on. I feel deeply in love.

When Betty and Dad discussed wanting to exchange houses Carl asked me to marry him. My father thought it was opportunistic for him-to just suddenly ask me to marry; he thought that Carl had no appreciation for what I brought to the relationship.

Of course, at that time I did not realize all of that but marrying me provided funds for his car, a home with a devoted wife and respectful family. I wanted to be with him-and moving into a different house took me away from the bad memories.

Carl gave me his all attention, he was tender, gentle and careful. In the beginning he had my back and understood where I was coming from and my hurt. When he first touched my hand—his touch made me feel alive and loved. When we married and he began …all I wanted was to be his. It was like a magical gift."

She continued "The move to Chicago opened my eyes. It brought to life how opportunistic, unappreciative, and selfish he was, but I denied the feelings. At that time Carl had no money of his own. His money barely paid his school bills. Carl put the house in Chicago in both of our names. He could have communicated about his desire to leave his medical group before sending out resumes. He could have discussed the type of opportunity he needed. He could have come to me and gently discussed why he did the things if he did, he would have made things better for all of us; he did not, and he just went ahead to do everything he wanted.

My father did not think that right. Carl and I went to counseling and each time he was asked to face something he did or said and apologize or explain. Instead, he just wanted the councilor to "fix me."

Genuinely, unconditional love was not there. He did not put himself into it unless it was something he needed.

I was unhappy- the entire family knew things were not good after we moved."

"You will forgive me Aunt Rita-but you still sound in love with Uncle Carl and from what I have heard about your relationship it was not what it appeared to be or what you hoped it would be. What happened? Ava asked.

"There was too much too soon it is hard to explain—Carl was struggling he really needed help to carry out his financially goals and, as a doctor, and his goal of finding better burn creams -- this played into our getting married.

The opportunity to pay for his schooling, have a car and to do whatever it was that he wanted to make himself a success was before him. He was not opposed to anything but just wanted what he wanted. He liked me, helped me and was comfortable with me; our family was appreciative of him, and he was again comfortable with them.

Years later, I realized what blind faith was and understood that most times it is unwarranted. Carl did not give me his heart.

Oh, in the beginning Carl would bring flowers occasionally and spend time understanding my issues; he tried to have my back. One councilor told me; Carl and I met at a time when we each needed each other. I needed him to help me get over the rape and to have someone to love-he needed someone to help him accomplish what he wanted--that was to be a success. Since he was the success, he sees it as having done it all on his own. And until that belief changes and I am not going to have what I thought I had. Looking at our situation now I look for him to have a revelation and tell me how much he appreciates me taking care of everything even working so he was free to accomplish his dreams. He needs to appreciate the relationship and what it has done and to want to continue together.

However, when Carl announced he would be moving into an apartment I realized all was lost; hope of romance, caring and emotional attachment would never happen. Carl made up his mind to be indifferent, uncaring and unloving and not to love me again-if indeed he did at one point.

But he is kind and in many ways. When I think back, I was the one in love--with love. "But Aunt Rita— how did," Rita interrupted "Ava, no one thing changes a relationship- trivial things increase and erode differences. When Carl would say or do something that hurt my fellings instead of discussing it and coming to a resolve, we would both zone out. We would let things go pretending they did not happen. We both did that from the start. I was not willing to stand up for myself he refused to argue. I just wanted to be with him and let it all pass.

In his family no one ever appreciated anyone expressing the need for constructive communication; they just pointed out issues. Carl would say he never wanted to hear a person's opinion-let alone give his "everything always changes." He was correct life evolves and new things are discovered and new thoughts on subjects appear.

Science is not an exact it depends on who is interpreting the issue that depends on their background and feeling, experience and schooling. Many doctors see just one way to heal something whereas other doctors know there may be many solutions. That is why we have homeopathic medicine.

"But Rita, we should all learn; when things are not worked out resentment grows. Issue feed resentment. The longer resentment and dislike hold one back from communicating and resolving differences and doing self- evaluation the longer and higher a wall comes between people." Greta said.

"I used to believe that marriage was a "safe" haven. That if you had an argument or disliked something-you would and could continue to work on it until it was resolved. Bur, Carl's understanding of being married was letting him make all the decisions to make him feel like a man." Rita added.

"But what about the other half of this relationship." Ava Asked. Rita said "I had a lot of questions: Who am I? Am I to be just a cheer leader? A puppet who nods when you ask to confirm? Who should I be? That's ok for him but that does not acknowledge me. If the man must decide everything-he doesn't need a wife-just a birthing person if he wants children and a maid for the things that need taking care of to make life comfortable. I contributed to his success in many ways. The bible points out that a woman was made to help man."

She continued "He is exceptionally good at communication and because he understands people he could make any situation a win-win. It was like a game. I loved and love, him to this day. I always felt staying together and hoping things would get better would be rewarded in time. But Carl kept a secret about his interview in Chicago-that was difficult to accept. Instead of discussing his issues with me he felt comfortable talking about his feeling more with others. Carl does not share my assessment of things or consider my questions and concerns." They took a break for a cup of tea and a cookie.

"Then, after we moved to Chicago, Carl won awards for his work. That is the reason why he is sought after for lectures today. He has proved his ideas and programs of treatment for burns work because they were approved by the US government and are being used all over the world. He discusses his theories, authors books and lectures. He had a challenging time years ago and everyone wanted Carl to bend-he did not and won."

"As years went by there was the night George died –I thought—Carl made passionate love to me. He held me in his arms, kissed me and was ever so gentle and loving. I was heaven.

Then things changed again. When Carl delivered Katherine and Joseph Carl, he went away on the lecture circuit for six years. I wanted independent children who could manage any-thing life dropped in their lap. It was all left to me, the house, the children, my job, the school issues, helping him with his office parties and so much more."

"Again, Aunt Rita you stayed together-why didn't you want to leave him? You could have taken the kids and left. You could have had a life with someone that would have liked and loved you who appreciated your abilities..." Rita interrupted

"You are correct Ava I could have done all that. But divorce would have been hard on the children, the family and hard on me. Children tend to love both their parents to separate them would have been putting them in a situation where they had no choice. How could I do that to myself-to my children, to the man I love who did not leave me when I was raped but helped me? To deny the children their father who loved them very much. There is more to life that just romance in the bedroom-there is being kind to one another, being used to one another's ways, doing things together, doing little deeds for one another, and being safe with someone -knowing that person is still a good person. Carl and I went through a tough time. My heart was broken I was devastated. I always felt rejected and depressed in time it effected my health. Consequently, when Carl said he was beginning a new project I was determined to change my expectations. I made up my mind then not to give anyone the power to hurt or demean me ever again.

I admit there were times I wanted to be in his arms and feel his kisses. I cried by myself. I knew I would never leave the marriage. I needed to accept a new form of peace and accept the companionship together we were able to have. That was when I wrote to Betty that I am not alone any longer. I released all the hurt that tormented me and choose peace. God has given me strength."

"Aunt Rita-did you ever have a boyfriend a lover?" Ava excitedly asked. "No Ava I did something better. I allowed myself to change an appreciate my own worth and values. You see honey I learned that forgiveness brings pleasure and freedom to the heart. It empowers one; I gave myself the gift of appreciating me and the ability to forgive. I changed my thinking, my attitude, and my heart. I decided to enjoy the good times that come; we still talk to each other, go out to dinner, enjoy our children, even have fun together. We also enjoy time alone together and that is a comfort.

I stayed working and keeping the twins around me. As the time, the twins were older; I had remade my thinking to understand that -- romance is for the young and life is for the rest of us.

I love Carl and love being with him. We are at ease with each other. His smile, to this day, lightens up my heart. I would never let him know my feelings since he does not feel the same. I shall enjoy the time we have together. I accept it for what it was worth. Years ago, I found an anonymous poem that went something like this:
"When you are driving on a journey and night falls, and you do not know how the road turns that is ok because that is when the stars come out, and you will see."

Rita added, "God is and has been my strength for a long time. I know Carl is a good man-he is committed to our family. In any marriage it may not always be what one thinks or hopes but if there is kindness, consideration and loyalty it is a relationship. Carl does not worry about anything. I just do what I can. I feel hope because God never gives up on anyone.

The ladies had lunch and Rita continued: "We are still together. If he wanted to be divorced, he would do it."

Chapter 74

Life so Easy

"Well ladies we have just a few more days in Rome –what shall we do?" Ava answered, "How about we just continue to talk about life?" Greta and Rita looked at each other and their gestures identified that decision was fine with them. "Who should begin?" Rita asked. "Well since you started this whole thing why don't you continue where you left off" Ava said.

"Fine, there is more to understand about the family-and just a little more about my prayers. You see I feel Carl's loneliness and frustration. He tries to drown himself in work and he purports to be happy, but no man is happy alone.

I just wait patiently and in time it will happen. But if he is getting an apartment. I want him to be happy—I still love the man I married. True love always wants what is best for the other person."

She continued "Ladies a one-sided love really hurts. But religion gives a renewed strength. I am resolved that we will always be a family and that in the end--all of us would be ok whether he finds another or not.

Chapter 75

Much Still to Learn

"Carl is living with me and being there-is really his way of loving. There is the theory "I give you deeds not words."
When a man enjoys the lifestyle of being together it gives him the freedom from life's challenges to work on — his own dreams--that is what I provide him.

Carl is such a successful businessman he could talk business all night expecting a woman to just sit there and listen. Instead of enjoying the diversity of each other and pulling it all together as a package. It is difficult to explain.

When Carl loves he is gentle, kind, thoughtful, caring and when he chooses not to love- he is indifferent, silent, expression less and not interested. I have survived both but if he moves out, I will find a way to survive the separation. I love Carl but I would want to take the high road. It would be a deeper understanding, and acceptance of someone else's needs; whether husband, wife or parent-we must always allow happiness and growth."

"Carl and I would still love our family; and be there for them. Carl taught me many things during our years together - about how forgiveness and how important it is, and that life is not a dream but reality we do not live in a dream world.

Your great grandma Betty once that "if someone you love had lost a leg-or was ill-would you leave them? She said, "Loving does not stop just because there is another kind of issue. In a normal relationship people would work on it together-but what if one could not? If one could not do you just give up? Would you think of yourself and abandon that person who showed you how to really love? That would be abandoning your integrity for your own selfishness. I believe that is why in a marriage we say, "for better or worse. I think Betty was right." Rita continued

"If you think of love like a story book romance-you will be disappointed in no time. Two people who marry should become one-but that becoming is the difficulty. If we think of love as a feeling –we will suffer the same disappointment all the time. We need to realize that feelings can change from minute to minute; but if we look at love as a "choice of commitment" then it may survive." Everything in life is a choice-do we weaken or grow stronger within ourselves. I have grown stronger, and I know Carl has. That is why when he said if the house is sold, he would get an apartment my answer was "OK."

Because you can never hold someone that does not want to be held."

This time it was Greta that spoke "Rita, what is love if you cannot acceptance and understand diversity, if one does not agree to work on issues? Is not love when each want - what is **best** for the other-without resentment, anger, indifference, frustration, and belittling? What happens when one person shines and does not allow the other to enter that persona and have their minutes of success?

"Ava's father loved us so much he wanted not only to show me love but he gave us everything he had out of love." This was the first time Ava heard her mother talk of her father in that way and she was taken back. "Mom did you love my father?" Ava asked. "Your father was the best thing that happened to me and the best man I have ever known—yes Ava when I think of true love, I think only of him." Ava went over and kissed her mother who was now in tears.

Rita then said "You see Ava-part of love is an understanding of the other person, accepting, forgiving, growing, expressing, communicating, caring and looking forward to your tomorrows together. Hope is that looking forward to for those things with understanding, acceptance and enjoying the differences of each other; this is the true meaning of "becoming" one. Nothing and no one are ever perfect- it is-just a choice to go on and to have the attitude and appreciation of acceptance-- that is really what is most important"

The ladies left Rome two days later. This ended up being a five month "trip" in Rome. Still, they all had a better understanding of their own feelings toward love— coupled with a deeper love for Rita sharing her experiences and philosophies.

Chapter 76

Happened That Way

Rita returned to Chicago and when their house was sold, she moved into her new place. Carl moved in the apartment near the airport. In fact, nothing appeared changed. Carl found a companion for about six weeks. Then one evening there was a knock-on Rita's door.

It was Carl, Rita invited him in and perked coffee. She told Carl she had a piece of apple cinnamon cake if he would like with his coffee. He said that he would enjoy that and thanked her.

Then Carl said, "Rita, I -I do not like living in the apartment despite it being close to the airport. I realize I am not happy traveling anymore. I would like to have you in my life. You have been my wife for almost forty years.

I am tired-tired of traveling and living in hotels and out of a suitcase.

Now there are videos that work for lectures. Going home to an empty apartment is lonely and being with another woman is not the same.
You and the kids are my family; I really want my family back. I have everything I set out to do but it means nothing if I do not have you with me."

Rita was shocked but answered, "Carl there is so much in our past that is …" He stopped her and said, "Rita, I know but that does not mean our future needs to be hindered by it if we still love and trust each other.

You were in Rome an exceptionally long time, and I missed you and love you and our family very much. I want us all to be together. Will you take a chance on me again?

Rita responded, "Carl are you sure-because…" "I promise you Rita we will be in love and together forever. We are living the last part of our lives and I want to share my whole life with you-could you find it in your heart to forgive me for the past and not turn me away from our future." Carl was in tears and so was Rita they kissed, and Carl spent the night. They showed each other how much they loved being together. Carl moved into the house with Rita that next Saturday. Everyone was overjoyed.

After Ava moved to Chicago, she was asked to meet an attorney who was teaching at Northwestern Law school. She laughed when Grant came into the room. She said "I don't understand Grant. Have you decided to teach now? Grant said that her Aunt Rita's educational changes will open the door to challenges. I investigated everything and decided we will need more attorneys to fight issues. The chancellor of Northwestern Law School was at a meeting one day, he offered me a teaching position for one course, and I took it and liked it. Teaching was less stressful than building an empire. Why not go to law school and see what you think.

Ava had been thinking about enrolling in Law school. She and Grant have so much in common and she was tired of teaching. She was just in time for classes to begin in September. Ava was always a great student and with Grant available to help her why not.

As was her way-Ave completed in two years and one semester. With a straight "A" average she was permitted to take as many courses as she could handle each semester. Graduating magna cum laud. Grant helped her study for the bar exam and on the day, notice came in of Ava passing the Chicago bar exam; Grant asked her to marry him.

They had a beautiful wedding in the Chicago Temple with Greta, Michael, Nora and all of Rita and Carl's family including Shana, David and their four children; Katherine, Jeff; Mary Jane and Jeffery Charles with their wives and all their four children. Joseph Carl and his three children attendance. It was a beautiful wedding service; they had a fabulous dinner in China Town with limos for the wedding party meeting at the acclaimed "Cuisines of China" restaurant. As a special gift to his bride Grant gave them a two-month honeymoon touring China.

After their marriage, Grant and Ava settled down on the magnificent mile in a beautiful condominium just built. They were able to design their 5000 square foot penthouse; each having their own office. They became a successful team. Grant and Ava became true sole mates. Their second year Ava learned they would be having their first set of twins: Graydon and Harrison. The boys were her pride and joy.

Then three years later their second set of twins were born Juliana, and Mariyah. Their family was complete. As the children were born Grandma Greta came to live with the family. Greta's first book was on raising children.

Ava continued to write in her spare time—this time children's books. Greta passed away at age 90, she never married. Michael and Nora lived at the retirement home for a total of nine years Nora passed away first and Michael died just two weeks later. They were in their late 80's both passed away in their sleep.

Greta was there for her parents and her relationship with her father became more loving and understanding. They loved their new home and were incredibly happy in the retirement home.

By the time of Ava and Grant's wedding Rita and Carl were helping Joseph and his new wife in the building they all bought, enjoying grandchildren.

Prologue:

How we live our Life is a choice—our emotions, feelings and attitudes come down to a commitment to our souls and our integrity.

We are the people we want to become—it is the becoming that requires continual commitment.

Prayer

Please Help me Lord:

I want to be happy within myself.
I want to feel the love and respect I so desire.
I want to see my dreams come to fruition.
Please help me, Lord!
I love you LORD,
Please guide me to see what
to do in all circumstances.

I want to bring {keep} our family together
always
I want to be happy within myself.
I want our children to feel the same way
Please help me, Lord!
Teach the beautiful children to
Understand, love; to respect,
and to be guided by you.
Committed to each other
Help them to be examples of kindness,
Compassion and understanding.
Give them the tools to have influence
In all the lives they touch.
Help them to love you, Lord,
every day of their lives.
Help me to understand your direction and
To appreciate the challenges, you put be-
fore me
as I learn your ways Lord
put me on your path.
Please help me, Lord!"

S. Marshall Kent

About the Author

S. Marshall Kent is retired. Spending twenty years in government employ after retiring as a teacher and principal.

Kent traveled extensively stopping in, China, Hong Kong, Istanbul, Philippians,Italy, Switzerland, Germany and more along with travel in the US and Canada.The characters and incidents in this book are a products of the author's imagination.

Clayton New York is used fictitiously. The authors strives to identify the need for deep difficult communication, coupling that communication with understanding a person's intent, feelings and situations, hope and if need be their background.

Spelling is also a form of communication. There may be other misspelled words in this book. Words said are hard to forget-but written words leave a legacy!

Good relationship require much work and thinking to understand how what we do is really perceived.

Printed in the United States
by Baker & Taylor Publisher Services